DOROTHY
DANDRIDGE

Dorothy Dandridge

An Intimate
Biography

An Original Holloway House Edition

Printed in the United States of America
Copyright © 1970, 1991, 1999 by Earl Mills

ISBN 0-87067-899-X
Holloway House Premiere Edition: August, 1999
COVER AND BOOK
DESIGN BY JESSE DENA

DOROTHY DANDRIDGE

An Intimate Biography

By

EARL MILLS

An Original Holloway House
Premiere Trade Edition
Holloway House Publishing Company
Los Angles, California

Ruby Dandridge, who had acting ambitions, and her daughters, Vivian and Dorothy. At the time Dorothy was four years old and had been performing at church socials for a year. When Vivian became jealous, Ruby developed an act for them called "The Wonder Kids" and fame quickly followed.

CHAPTER ONE

Dorothy Dandridge was born in Cleveland, Ohio on November 9, 1922. It has been said that she was twice cursed: she was born black and beautiful. Not in her lifetime would her country realize more than a pretense of equal rights. The Civil Rights movement was just beginning to gather steam when her sudden death shocked all of us who knew her and her thousands of fans around the world. In her own world her beauty and talent had allowed her to open many doors that remained firmly closed against most Black Americans.

As her manager and close friend, I was there to witness her greatest triumph and her deepest tragedy.

The ultimate triumph came on the night of March 30, 1955, the night of the televised Academy Awards telecast for work done in 1954. The presentation of the Oscars, in those days, was Hollywood's gift to the country, the nation's ultimate glamour event. And the telecast was still new, giving everyone a peek at those untouchable stars of motion pictures. Unlike now, there were no other awards shows of importance telecast. The Oscars were it.

Not only the biggest and best, but the only. Only a few short years before it would not have been possible to imagine the telecast nor the participation of a beautiful woman of color playing such as an important role as a nominee for Best Actress.

For a short time in the mid-1950s, the Oscar ceremony was telecast simultaneously from New York and Hollywood, a cumbersome idea that didn't last. 1955 was one of those times. The master of ceremonies was Bob Hope. The scenes were the RKO Pantages Theater in Hollywood and New York's NBC Century Theater, where Dorothy Dandridge, playing an engagement at the Waldorf-Astoria hotel, attended.

Backstage at the Century, the very beautiful and very nervous woman, the first woman of her race ever to be nominated for an Oscar in the "Best Actress" category, waited, petrified with fear. She had become the first black major movie star. As yet, she hadn't found the palliative for fright: alcohol. Later, in tragedy, she used it to contain all her emotions.

She was intimidated by her competition: Judy Garland, *A Star Is Born*, Grace Kelly, *The Country Girl*, Audrey Hepburn in *Sabrina* and Jane Wyman for *Magnificent Obsession.*

Dorothy insisted there was no way she could win. This was her way of convincing the fates that she deserved to win because she was so humble about it. Oh, how badly she wanted to win. That would be the ultimate victory.

Only days before named by a committee of expert photographers as one of the five most beautiful women in the world, she stood in a bright white-yellow satin gown backstage as a thing of eternal loveliness.

She had prayed she'd win. She had memorized her thank-you speech. But she said just before the rehearsals, "It's too soon for me to win. I'm too new in the movie business. If I don't win, I hope my friend Judy (Garland) wins it."

As an important star of motion pictures, television and nightclubs, she believed even if she lost she would eventually be an Oscar winner. So in the end she'd have her glory.

She held a small statuette in her hand which she'd present as the award for film editing. Jean Negulesco, Academy official, had pulled a neat trick; he got the big star nominees there by making them presenters. They had to show up.

Dorothy's disposition was such that she might not have appeared at New York's NBC Century Theater for fear of losing. But as a presenter she was forced to.

"It's a long way from the 'Wonder Children,'" she said to me nervously. She smiled. That was a sister vaudeville team she toured with when she was a child. She had earned $75,000 the past year and currently was the first Negro ever to appear at the plush Empire Room of the Waldorf-Astoria Hotel in New York. Those years she alone was stepping over the color line, in many ways, and soon others would follow.

Dorothy was the third black, and the first black female, to ever take part in an Academy Award show. In 1950 Dr. Ralph Bunche made the principal speech. In 1952 Billy Daniels sang the nominated song, "Because You're Mine."

She presented the editing award to Gene Milford for editing "On The Waterfront."

About this time the career crisis of a possible Oscar had enveloped her in a web of nerves. She watched spellbound while Elia Kazan got the directing award for *On The Waterfront*. Marlon Brando won the best actor award for the same picture.

And now the moment! Dorothy set her frozen

smile and crossed her fingers. Her sister Vivian and I were at her side.

Cool and handsome, William Holden walked on stage to make the presentation. He opened the envelope.Without any introductory remark he announced, "Grace Kelly for *The Country Girl.* Dorothy said to me, "I wish Judy had won it." She was terribly let down, yet so relieved. The pressure was off. Now she could relax. "Next time," she told herself. There would be be a next time. Marlon Brando came over and surprised her. He kissed her. A black kissed by a white. The curious showed surprise.

The Associated Press reported to the world-- "Dorothy Dandridge is a picture of loveliness as she attends the Academy Award presentations at New York's Century Theater. The gracious Dandridge stole the show at New York's version of the Academy Award ceremonies though movie stars and celebrities were a dime a dozen. Dot Dandridge currently is sensational at the Waldorf-Astoria. She literally wowed cafe society in her debut last week. The first Negro artist to appear at the exclusive hotel, the shapely thrush was hailed as one of the most beautiful and talented women ever booked into the Waldorf-Astoria's Empire Room." What a night of triumph.

Dottie Mae was living in the Waldorf Towers suite while performing at the Empire Room. General Douglas MacArthur and former President Herbert Hoover were her neighbors. Munching on a plate of chitlins late this Oscar night, delivered to her by a Harlem restaurant, Dottie said, "Earl, dear, I know I'm going to win an Oscar one day. I really enjoy acting and it will get me off the road. You know, I was here in New York working at the Cotton Club when I was fifteen and I later traveled everywhere with Cab Calloway, Duke Ellington, Jimmy Lunceford –

In 1955 Dorothy Dandridge became the first black actress ever nominated for the Best Actress Academy Award by the Academy. Her competition consisted of Grace Kelly, Judy Garland, Jane Wyman,and Audrey Hepburn. Dandridge was pulling for Marlon Brando to win Best Actor for On The Waterfront and when he did he kissed her, shocking many of the attendees.

as the Dandridge Sisters. I'll sure be glad to stay in one place for awhile."

"Angel face, I believe you really will win an Oscar. You were great as Carmen. The Times said, 'Carmen has the stamp of greatness'; and in California, Howard McClay wrote, 'To Miss Dandridge goes this reviewer's nod for one of the most exciting performances these eyes have ever seen, easily the best all-Negro film ever to come out of Hollywood.' Life, Time, Ebony, Our World, almost every important publication has praised your talents. You can't miss."

Otto Preminger, the director of *Carmen Jones,* based on the opera Carmen by Georges Bizet, was of the opinion that Dorothy Dandridge was far too "lady like" to act a convincing Carmen (reset in the 1940s), a woman of the streets--more or less. On her third audition she showed up dressed somewhat similar to the figure pictured in the photograph opposite, swinging her hips and flirting--and was immediately tested for the role--and hired that day. It would bring her an Academy nomination for Best Actress, the first black woman to be so honored.

Dorothy Dandridge and Harry Belafonte in a scene from Carmen Jones. At the time, Miss Dandridge thought that this would be the beginning of a long and prosperous career in films, especially after the Motion Picture Academy

nomination for Best Actress. However, she would only do one more film that would be considered "major" and that was *Porgy and Bess* with Sidney Pointier, with whom it is said she got along better than with Belafonte.

Dorothy Dandridge at a teenage party in 1941. At the time the Dandridge Sisters (Dorothy, Vivian, and Etta Jones) were already stars. Two years before they had been featured at the New York Copa with the Nicholas Brothers.

CHAPTER TWO

The blackest, most tragic day in Dorothy Dandridge's young life happened seven years after her historic triumph. It was a damp, foggy day in November 1962.

In the second year after she married Harold Nicholas of the dancing Nicholas Brothers in 1942, a wedding attended by, among other Hollywood black celebrities, Hattie McDaniel, Dorothy gave birth to her one and only child. They named the little girl Harolyn.

To Dorothy it was truly a miracle. She always thought of herself as being less than capable, and not productive, almost worthless. The fact that she was able to give birth to a baby was a genuine miracle, to her. But there she was with a beautiful baby girl.

The child turned out to be retarded.

During the first year after the birth, Dorothy went from doctor to doctor, from psychiatrist to psychiatrist, from hospital to hospital. She refused to believe the brain damage was incurable. She refused to accept the verdict of "no hope."

She appealed to her family, her church, her doctors. Why? Why had it happened to Lynn and her? There were no answers. What had she done wrong? She came up with this reason for her retarded daughter. The night her labor pains started she refused to go to the hospital until her husband came home. He'd taken their only automobile to play golf that day.

The pains were coming closer and closer together and still she refused to go without her husband. In the end, she had to go with a girl friend because he still hadn't shown up. She got there just in time to deliver the baby in a bed. Some thoughtless person told her this was the cause of the brain damage. It is far-fetched but perhaps that might be the reason. The other reason, she was told, was that she may have moved during the delivery and the forceps damaged the little girl's head. No matter how it happened, she felt guilty and depressed, and blamed herself as the reason for her little girl's retardation.

In later years Dorothy was to team with Jacqueline Kennedy in a concerted effort to help the retarded. She learned that mental retardation then afflicted 5,500,000 Americans, that victims of mental retardation can be helped and that the mentally retarded should be taught to live, as far as possible, useful lives. At the request of the White House, Dorothy recorded radio messages on behalf of the Joseph P. Kennedy, Jr. Foundation along with Dale Evans Rogers, Bette Davis, Pearl Buck and others. Dorothy's message was broadcast by almost 5,000 radio stations, according to Sargent Shriver.

But for years the tragedy of a retarded child was a blot on her life.

This day, late in 1962 while Dorothy, in very poor health, was arranging for her divorce and bankruptcy, a careless doctor dropped off Harolyn (age 17 with a mentality of four-year-old) at Dorothy's doorstep. When Dorothy opened the door, Lynn rushed past her mother without recognizing her and with one finger extended at the piano she played the same note over and over for hours. Dorothy stood there, pity and shock registered on her still beautiful face. Then she wept uncontrollably. Harolyn didn't stop playing her one note for a moment.

The telephone rang. It was Dorothy's attorney. He had studied Dorothy's fast fading financial empire and could see no way out other than bankruptcy. She had to get rid of her home, two automobiles; she owed an awesome $127,994.90 to seventy-seven creditors, all incurred during her three year marriage to Jack Dennison.

She owed hotels, travel agencies, banks, doctors, utility companies, laundries, pharmacies and super-markets. In 1959 when Dorothy married Jack Dennison she was earning a quarter of a million a year. Dennison, a Canadian of Greek descent, was born in Montreal in 1912. He moved to New York in 1934 and was employed at both the Waldorf-Astoria and the Astor hotels before moving to Los Angeles three years later. He served in the U. S. Navy during World War II and moved to Las Vegas in the early 1950s not long after Bugsy Segal awakened that sleepy little Mormon town to the possibilities of his dream of building the gambling capital of the world. Dennison eventually worked as a maitre d' at the Flamingo, the original gambling casino, and then moved to its first rival, the then new El Rancho, and finally to the still newer Riviera, where he first met Dorothy. At the time she was on the rebound from an off and on relationship with the director of *Carmen Jones*, Otto Preminger, and was receptive to Dennison's courtship which seems to have been rather calculated. He sent her flowers after every performance and went out of his way to see that she was comfortable. Later he visited her in Los Angeles.

Nicknamed "the Silver Fox," he was tall, dark, handsome and always well-groomed--and a very sympathetic listener. In spite of his reputation as being a womanizer at least on par with Harold Nicholas, she soon eloped with him.

It was rumored among her friends that Dorothy was leaving herself open to being used by the vain charmer. She backed him financially in a club and restaurant venture. He was able to persuade her to back his business ventures by telling her it was, always, in the best interest of her and Lynn. For instance, her told her she could give up going on the road to perform at clubs if he had his own in Hollywood where she would be able to perform when she desired and while waiting for film offers.

The club quickly became a disaster, mostly because of Dennison's lack of management experience. In his demands for more and more financial aid, he exhibted a cruel violent streak that kept her on edge. By the third year of the marriage, in 1962, worry had affected her health. Her assets were gone, her health was diminished, her income shrinking. There had been many bad investments. It was an extremely unhappy woman who was suddenly faced with the unexpected teenager and the one note serenade.

The saddest part of all was that there was no money left for the private care of her mentally retarded daughter. Lynn would have to be committed to a state institution. Dorothy was in shock.

While Lynn continued to play her note, a copy of Dorothy's divorce papers against Jack Dennison arrived in which she accused Dennison of extreme cruelty, claiming he struck her on many occasions. She asked no alimony but said she and her husband had mutual debts "incurred principally for the benefit of the defendant." She requested he pay $14,600 on such debts.

During her marriage to Dennison, Dorothy started to drink heavily, take many kinds of pills, lose her health, lose her money and become less and less successful in her career as each month passed.

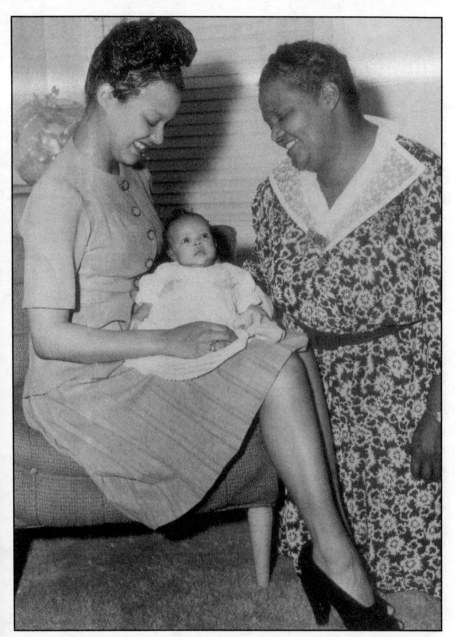

Dorothy with baby Harolyn and mother Ruby in happier days two years after she married Harold Nicholas of the famed Nicholas Brothers dancing team.
Soon after the baby was born the marriage was on the rocks as Harold didn't really enjoy being a husband nor a father.

Dorothy Dandridge and her daughter, Harolyn. The infant was born retarded and Dorothy always blamed herself, even though she was told over and over by doctors that it was not her fault The child never advanced past the intelligence of a four year old.

CHAPTER
THREE

I'm quite sure that if Dorothy had appraised her life carefully, she would have chosen her childhood years as the best.

Those were carefree days, as she often said, when she didn't know the difference between black and white.

If a psychiatrist did anything for her it was to bring back the nostalgia by probing and probing. He made her see and relive her childhood again and so her memories were sharp for the retelling.

"You know what my sister Vivian did," she laughed gaily, "when I was six years old? Well, she saved her pennies and wanted to give me a birthday present. She bought me a pint of ice cream and on the way home she became intrigued with some of her friends skipping rope and by the time she got to me and presented me with the ice cream, and I opened it, it was all liquid mush. When I started to cry, she said, 'Oh, all you have to do is put it in the ice box and it'll be good ice cream again.'"

Then Dorothy would laugh and laugh in the telling, "I then took it and put it in the ice box and then every twenty minutes we looked to see if it had hardened. Long before it had completely jelled, we went to the ice box and got it out and ate it. It was one of the best birthday presents I've ever received.

" I don't think I was more than eight when Vivian bought me a fur piece that fit around the neck. Of course it was artificial and second hand and worn, and probably didn't cost more than fifty cents.

"I looked at it bewilderedly and asked what it was and Vivian explained it to me in luscious terms, telling me that only the most important and rich women wore such a neck piece. 'But,' I asked practically, 'What am I going to do with it?'

"Said Vivian, repeating after me, 'What are you going to do with it? You're going to wear it on Sunday when you go to church.'

"That satisfied me at the time but I don't remember ever wearing it. I remember I tried it on and it looked awfully like I had a dead cat around my neck. So I hid it. Whenever Vivian asked what I had done with her beautiful fur piece, I said I was saving it for the proper occasion. Of course, the proper occasion never came.

"One night when there was a party next door and it was cold out, Vivian found it somewhere and insisted I wear it, and I did, but the moment I got into the party I took it off and stuck it into my overcoat pocket. No one was going to find me with that around my neck."

Dorothy laughed and laughed about it. "Earl," she said, "you know I've had the most beautiful mink and beaver pieces since then but none made the impact that that straggly piece of fur made on my birthday."

Dorothy's life seemed to be just flashing pictures of gaiety and happiness. She had very few unpleasant memories. Then why was she so confused and defensive and unhappy?

I suppose there's no answer to that.

She had one teacher she was crazy about. I think it was in the third grade. Her name was Miss Roach and she was a colored lady of indeterminate years. She had never married and she loved all her children, all the children in her classes.

She chose Dorothy to come home with her one day and have cookies and tea and then help her put up an aerial for her new radio. This was a great honor and Dorothy was very proud, only unhappy that she hadn't dressed for the occasion.

They went to Miss Roach's home, which was a neat little two-story white cottage. They first had their tea and cookies . The cookies were all homemade and they had walnuts on top of them, making each cookie look like a face. Dorothy was fascinated by them and also by the beautiful cushions Miss Roach had around the house. Each one had a message of love on it.

Then they went on the roof and strung the wire from the clothes pole down through the window to the radio, but the radio didn't work. Miss Roach tried everything. She worked on the aerial and shook the radio, and then she said she thought it might be the tube.

Dorothy continued, "So both of us went down to the store and the man at the store thought it was a condenser. Miss Roach had just enough money to pay for the condenser and on the way home she apologized for not taking me in for ice cream."

Dorothy, who had ten cents in her pocket, insisted that she treat Miss Roach and Miss Roach allowed her to. It was one of the most magnificent gestures of Dorothy's life to be able to pay for the ice cream cones, and Miss Roach knew it.

It made Dorothy feel ten feet tall and when the radio played once more and Miss Roach tuned to concert music, along with the memory of the ice cream cones and the treat, Dorothy was divinely happy.

When Dorothy and Vivian were very young, their mother bought them a pet parrot. Whatever possessed her to do that, Dorothy didn't know. But one day there was the parrot in a huge cage hung from a nail on the wall.

"But what will we do with it?" Dorothy asked.

And her mother said, "You teach it to speak."

From then on, Vivian and Dorothy stood for hours talking and singing but not a peep from the parrot. This went on for several days until Dorothy told her mother she didn't think that the parrot could talk.

Ruby, her mother, insisted that the tradesman said it could talk and if he said so, there was no doubt that it could talk.

So Ruby started talking to the parrot and that didn't work. Then they thought maybe a male voice would do it and Ruby brought in John, one of Dot's little friends. John stood in front of the parrot and said, "Hello there," and the parrot immediately replied, "Hello there."

Everyone was dumfounded and then they started giggling and laughing and rolling around on the floor while the parrot repeated, over and over, "Hello there." Every time he said it, they burst out with fresh laughter.

It seems the parrot before had a male owner and women's voices meant nothing to him, but when John said things he could imitate several of them. It was a great discovery. John then became almost a member of the household and the parrot was around for several years.

In time, John's place was taken by several other boys, but never would the parrot imitate a girl. Somehow it struck both Vivian and Dorothy funny and they just loved that parrot.

Dorothy told me she often would be called upon to take care of neighbors' babies. It wasn't like it is today where the kids charge. Dorothy did it for fun and as a lark. She always loved children. Even though she was a child herself at the time, she was taking care of children not much younger than she was. Because of those children, she had a lot of happy stories to tell.

One little girl that she baby-sat dressed in her mother's white gingham dress without Dorothy knowing what she was doing. The child tripped and fell down the stairs into a coal pile. When she came upstairs, the dress was smudged and black with coal dust. Dorothy and the little girl set about trying to clean it. They washed it and ironed it and it was just finished when the little girl's mother came home.

She was a sort of flighty young woman who had no husband—no visible husband, that is . She said hello to the two children and then looked at the dress and said, "Oh, I see Mrs. Margaret came back." Mrs. Margaret was the washerwoman. And she just put the dress away, never knowing the difference.

Once Dorothy was a heroine lauded by the neighborhood. She was minding a child who went into the second floor bathroom and locked himself in. Dorothy tried to get the little one to open it and banged on the door, but she couldn't do anything about it. So Dorothy went to the garage and got a ladder. While other people watched, she climbed up the ladder and squeezed in through the little bathroom window and then, of course, was able to open the door.

One day Dorothy was in the house with a cousin, a cute little boy about three years of age. They were in the house alone when a photography salesman came around. He took one look at Dorothy and the little boy and said, "You'd make wonderful subjects for our pictures. Do you know with our pictures you might get into the movies and become famous? Where's your mother, little girl? I want to talk to her."

Dorothy said, "Mother isn't home but I can give you permission."

"No," the man said. "We have to have permission from an adult or we can't shoot pictures."

"Well," Dorothy said, acting very grown up, "isn't there something I can sign?"

"No," the man insisted. "You have to be older. But I'll leave these papers with you and you tell your mother to sign them and we'll make both of you famous."

By this time the little boy was clamoring that he wanted to be famous, too. When the salesman came back a few days later, the little boy was gone but Dorothy had signed the papers where her mother was supposed to sign. A few pictures were taken of her and then delivered. Dorothy got hell when the pictures were delivered with the bill, but Ruby paid. From that time on the rules were that Dorothy was never to sign for anything again, especially not sign her mother's name.

Dorothy loved her childhood, was childlike all her life and loved children. It was a cruel trick of fate to give her one child that was mentally unwell. Of course, the question had to be asked, why didn't she have other children?

She had the opportunity of having more. I suspect that deep down Dorothy was afraid another child would be that way and maybe another and she couldn't get up the courage to do anything about that.

Dorothy remembered an incident that happened at the beach, which gave her adult self more of an insight into her childhood self. She and some friends were playing in the sand, building castles and moats and having a world of fun on a beautiful summer day when one of the children came up with what looked like a little diamond. It was apparently a piece of glass but they all shrieked and ah'd and ooh'd in excitement. When they showed it to Ruby she went along with it and said how marvelous it was to find a beautiful diamond. The thing was about as big as a fingernail and wet sand stuck to it.

The kids were in seventh heaven talking about how they would sell it and buy this and that. Ruby paid no more attention to them. Then a man in bathing trunks came walking along the beach and said to the kids, "What's all the excitement?"

Dorothy showed him the diamond. The man was obviously kind, held it up to the sun and said, "I'd like to buy this from you. How much would you sell it for?"

Dorothy said, "A hundred million dollars."

The man said, "I don't have that amount with me but maybe we can make a deal anyway."

Dorothy and the children got off to the side and one of the girls said, "All white men are rich, so we should charge him a lot."

Dorothy never forgot that--all white men are rich. She believed it for awhile, too.

Then they went back to the man and they made a deal. He gave them fifty-five cents for it. Of course, he was just being a nice fellow and I'm sure he threw it away after he gave them the money.

The kids were very happy. Fifty-five cents was real. Several million was just a figure. They immediately ran to the ice cream stand to spend their money gains and the man went off whistling.

One of Dorothy's favorite stories was "A Perfect Day for Banana Fish" by J. D. Salinger. She used to tell me she loved the story because it was close to another incident that happened to her on the beach when she was small.

The kids would always see this one man who would be lifted down to the beach and put in a little metal wheelchair. His legs were much smaller than the average person's and obviously were paralyzed and useless. He'd sit in the sun. He was very tan and good looking. He would read and watch the children play. One time the children were playing volleyball and the ball rolled near his chair.

All the children were afraid to go get it, but Dorothy finally got up courage enough to walk slowly to the chair and ask permission from the man to pick it up. He smiled and said, "But be careful, young lady. That's no ball. That's a bomb. It might go off."

She paid no attention and brought it back to the children but then she thought that was very odd and, to her young mind, very interesting. After the game she walked slowly back to the man and asked him his name.

He said he had never been given a name but he was thinking of taking one soon. To her that was perfectly all right and she told him her name.

"Dorothy Dandridge. Do you know," he mused, "people that have the same initials in their first and last names are called something, though I forget what. But it is very lucky."

Dorothy beamed.

He said, "I take it that you are last year's Miss America, because you're very beautiful and you're on the beach as one of the prizes."

Dorothy was at the age where she accepted everything literally and explained to the man, "No, I'm not Miss America," and it was just that her mother had taken her to the beach. Dorothy asked him what he did.

"What," the man said, "you don't recognize the President of the United States when you see him?"

"Are you really?" Dorothy asked.

"Of course," the man said. "I left my badge in my hotel, but I am."

Dorothy was very impressed.

"Is there anything you want that I can have done for you?" the man asked.

Dorothy thought for a while. "Well, yes. My mother needs a new pail. You know, for scrubbing."

The man looked puzzled. "Well," he said, "that's the most difficult thing in the world to replace and I don't know if I can handle it, but when I get back to Washington, I'll pass a law so that you can get a new pail. Would you give me your address?"

Dorothy gave him the address.

"Ah," he said, "I recognize that address. That's where the London Castle used to be before the water came in.

Dorothy was puzzled by that.

"Of course," the man said, "you know that the world is all mixed up . That this used to be Europe and Europe used to be the United States."

Dorothy said she hadn't taken geography yet in school and the man said, "What a shame."

Then Dorothy asked, "Are you happy?"

"No, I'm not happy," the man said slowly. "It has nothing to do with me but with the world. You see, people aren't kind . People don't love each other."

"But I love you," Dorothy said.

"I'm taking that as a proposal of marriage," the man said suddenly, breaking the mood, "and I accept."

"You mean you want to marry me?" Dorothy asked.

"More than that," the man said. "There's nothing I want more in the whole world."

"Well," Dorothy said, "I don't think my mother would let me . I think I'm too young."

"I will present my case to your mother later in the day and then we will plan an international wedding feast."

Dorothy now seemed uncomfortable. She said, "I think I have to go home."

"Well, we all have to go home sometime," the man said. "Soon they'll come to take me home, too, but I want to tell you this has been a very edifying and satisfactory time that we've had here and I hope we'll see each other again."

"Oh, I'm here every day during vacation," Dorothy said, "except when there are thunderstorms. I'm afraid of lightning."

"You are?" the man said. "That's just the Lord striking a match. You mustn't be afraid of that."

"But I am," Dorothy said, stubbornly. "But I'll be here every day that it doesn't lightning."

"Good," the man said, "then we have a date."

And Dorothy ran off.

Dorothy saw Joe Silver all through the summer. Several years later when she thought about him, she tried to find out who he was and what he did, but she never did find him . But he had considerable influence on her. A lot of what he said was gibberish and madness, but a lot was sensible. Somehow the gibberish and the madness passed over her head, but some of the sensible things stuck.

Joe told her she had much grace and that while clumsiness was a normal part of childhood, she didn't have it. He told her it was a sign from the Lord that she was meant to be a ballet dancer or just a plain ordinary dancer or singer or actress, that grace went with those professions. She listened wide-eyed. It was probably the first time that an adult had complimented her.

The difference between whites and blacks was bound to come up. Dorothy asked him, naively, whether he had always been white because to her it was all very confusing to have people of different colors.

"No," Joe said. "I've been several colors. But I think I like white the best because I can become lost in the sea of light. You see, with my other colors I'd be different and it's poison to be different in this world."

"But I'm different," Dorothy said.

"Yes," he said sadly, "but maybe some day you won't be."

She held on to that little grain of suggestion.

Always he had the same easy patter. With the ice cream man who passed once a day: "Son," he would say, though he was an old man, "I want the biggest ice cream bar you have. None of them small ones. I want it for this wonderful young lady." The man played the part well and went scrambling around in his plastic bag, filled with dry ice smoking away, looking for the largest ice cream bar in the world. Finally he came up with one.

He would say, "Here it is. I've been saving it for you."

Dorothy would dance delightedly and get the bar. "Is it really?" she asked. "The biggest bar in the whole world?"

"Yes," Joe said. "But soon it won't be. It'll be the biggest bar in a little girl's stomach in the whole world."

And Dorothy would laugh. "Why," she asked, "can't people be like an ice cream bar? Black on the out-side, the chocolate, and white on the inside, the ice cream?"

"It's a wonderful idea," Joe said, "and when I get back to the White House, I'll do something about it."

Dorothy felt that Joe could do anything, when in reality, he could do very little. He was crippled, para-lyzed from the waist down, and he had to wait for a hired man to carry him back to his hotel every day. Once, when it rained, Dorothy helped him push the chair back under the boardwalk, with Joe proclaiming, "Don't worry about me getting wet. To be dry is no pro-found state . Rain is blessed by heaven."

"Yes," Dorothy said practically, "but you get your clothes all damp and you feel terrible. And you might catch cold."

Joe said, "I'm too slow to catch anything, so don't you worry about that, young lady."

Joe expected her every day and would have little gifts for her. Then as the summer started to come to a close, she realized she wouldn't see him again and that made her very sad. "Where can I come to visit you when I go back to school?" she asked.

"I'm afraid that won't be possible," Joe said. "I need tests. Do you know what tests are?"

"Yes," she said. "You take them in class at the end of the term."

"Well, not exactly," he said, "but I'm going some-where in the Midwest this fall to a hospital and they're going to take tests. So I won't be available for consultations for some time. But let's say that next summer we'll meet here and every summer thereafter. And also, young lady, don't forget that we'll be married some day and so we'll see each other often."

That pleased Dorothy. "But sometimes I think you might be fooling me," she said.

"I never indulge in it," he answered. "There's not time in the world for fooling. It's a very serious world."

Every once in a while he'd pull out a harmonica and play for her and she'd request songs. He could play almost everything and could meet her requests. "Music," he told her, "makes you think; and think along the right paths. It's emotional, you know. Nostalgic. When you're thinking music, you never think hate or violence."

It was over Dorothy's head. She asked him, "When will you turn color again?"

"Why?" he asked.

"Because I want you to be the same color as I am."

"I wish I could," he responded. "Just for a trial period. It would give me more insight."

"Oh, no," Dorothy said, misinterpreting what he had said. "I like being black. All my friends are. It's just that I wanted you to be one of us. My mother is black, you know, and my father isn't living with us, but he was, too."

Joe looked long at Dorothy and said, "People that have handicaps, like you and me, are doubly blessed by the Lord. We were given them to make us more firm and more resilient. A burden gives one an opportunity to better study the world. So you should feel lucky."

"Do you?" Dorothy asked.

"Sometimes," Joe responded.

Then came the day. It was a Sunday, and Dorothy remembered it well when she told Joe the next day she had to go back to school so she wouldn't be on the beach.

Joe said, "It's hard for me to cry but if I could, I would. You're my best friend and I'm very sorry to see you go. And that's not nonsense. That's truth."

"I'm sorry, too," Dorothy said, and she did cry. Tears rolled down her face and Joe held her close to him.

"I'm going to grow up to be a famous actress," Dorothy said. "Or even a famous singer. Because you said I could be."

"Yes," Joe said. "You are right now, only you don't know it. But soon everyone will know it and when they do, you will know it too."

"Is that right?" Dorothy said. It was hard for her to imagine that she already had greatness. Then she asked, "When you're finished with your tests, do you go back to Washington?"

"Yes," he said. "I expect that they'll really need me after I'm away for a while. The world is in an awful mess."

"It is?" Dorothy asked. "But it's so nice down here. The beach is so clean and the sun is so nice."

"Yes," Joe said, "but that didn't come as an edict from Washington. That came from a higher place. I'm afraid our improvements don't compare to this."

Then Dorothy's friends came to get her and she kissed Joe on the cheek and he squeezed her hand.

He said, "Goodbye, little black girl. I love you truly."

She left. And she never saw him again, but she always remembered him because he was the first to say she would become a famous actress or a famous singer.

I knew Dorothy for many years. I always felt that she had an inner greatness. Much of it was caused by her own hardships.

One little twist one way or the other and she could have been one of the entertainment greats. Not that she wasn't important, but she could have been twice as big—three times. It wasn't her fault nor was it because of the fact that she was black. I think she handled that well. She was always a credit to her people.

When conditions hemmed her in and outside forces caused her to drink and take pills and fight with the only weapons that seemed to help, she still maintained that dignity. Things she did that she was ashamed of she hid behind closed doors. Very few people knew the panic that went on inside her.

When I think of Dorothy, I only think of the happy times. The gay times. When she re-enacted the character Julie from "Showboat" in the living room of friends. When she sang at a musicale. Her opening nights. The games on the beach in South America. The shopping excursions in Europe. Her awe the first time in New York. Her childish handling of money. The petty hates she had that disappeared with a kind word.

These are the things I think of.

She wasn't one to really display the drama within her. More often she'd skip over it. She was proud to be a Negro. She never thought in terms of color first. She liked good people and I believe she never understood men. She was almost always nervous, tense and involved with one crisis or another. She had her best times when she was cooking and talking for hours to someone she liked.

The young and "new Dorothy Dandridge" who decided she would have it all--marriage to Harold Nicholas, a family and her own career in show business. The marriage failed but she did make a career for herself, both in night clubs and films. By the early 1950s, She was as well known as Lena Horne.

Inspired by the success of the Andrew Sisters, mother Ruby decided the "Wonder Children" should move on to become the Dandridge Sisters and since there were three Andrew Sisters and also other girl groups made up of three, Ruby decided to hire Etta Jones (left) as the third sister.

The group became very popular and by the time Dorothy was fifteen, they were playing top clubs in the country. Eventually, Etta Jones decided she wanted to get married and leave the group. Later she returned to to show business and became a respected jazz artist.

Etta Jones, the "third" Dandridge Sister, in 1998, when she was a Grammy Nominee for Best Jazz Vocal Performance. The albumn, "My Buddy" was a tribute to the great band leader Buddy Johnson, with whom Etta started singing and touring at age 15, in 1944, with her parents permission.

CHAPTER FOUR

Dorothy grew up in an all-female world. Her father left the family before Dorothy's birth and Ruby Dandridge was forced to find a way of earning enough money to support her two daughters during the depths of the depression era.

Mrs. Dandridge was a devout woman and was very active in her church work. She was often called on to give recitations at the many church socials she and her daughters attended. One day Ruby felt ill on a day she was scheduled to give a recitation at church. Dorothy, who had always been a quiet child, spoke up and said she could do the recitation for her mother. She was three years old at the time.

Ruby challenged Dorothy to recite the speech she had been rehearsing. Much to Ruby's surprise, she repeated it to perfection, and again at the church social that evening. The church audiences found Dorothy so cute and charming that she was soon receiving requests for repeat performances. Her sister Vivian quickly became jealous of Dorothy's popularity and Ruby, naturally, understanding the situation, coached Vivian to perform.

And thus was born the Wonder Children. Their

reputation in the Baptist Church social circles grew rapidly. While Ruby worked as a cook in a restaurant, the Wonder Children performed in Cleveland churches. When the children were asked to perform at a Baptist convention in the South, Mrs. Dandridge accepted the invitation on the condition that only their travel expenses and food costs be paid.

Their success at the convention created a demand. Soon invitations were coming from both the South and midwest sectors of the African American world. Their popularity quickly grew to the point that Ruby had to give up her job to accept the many invitations for them to perform. As she had taught the children their repertoire and created the dances, she decided to charge for the group. She added a piano player, a female disciplinarian, to the troupe.

The Wonder Children toured Negro churches throughout the South for five years. Although these were school and play years for most children, Dorothy and Vivian were in show business, and while school was a hit and miss proposition, there wasn't much time to play. Then, in 1930, Ruby decided to migrate to sunny California.

Ruby had always dreamed of settling down in a permanent nest. She felt Los Angeles was the place. There was not much money but Ruby did manage to find them a $40 a month apartment that was comfortable enough.

The Wonder Children continued to perform for churches and benefits while they went to school. By the time Dorothy was age twelve she was starting to get small parts in pictures. She was pretty, friendly, likable and soon found it easy to get picture jobs.

Until then she only knew the Negro world. She had a fear of Caucasians. They were mysterious. She lived in the ghetto and only saw whites when she ventured into the movie studio world, where she often felt insecure. She was always happy to return to the ghetto after work.

When she was thirteen, the family lived in Watts. Dorothy was playing potsy with her girl friends. She bounced from one numbered chalk box to another, hopping on one foot and picking up the piece of chalk she used for a marker. She wore a white middie blouse with a black tie and black cotton skirt.

About ten feet away two white laborers stood idly watching the game. Dorothy overheard them. "The little black bitch who's jumping now. Yeah, that's the one. How'd you like to spin that on your pecker."

And the other one said, "Those black kids have venereal diseases from the day they're born. You can count me out."

To which the first commented, "As far as I'm concerned, it's worth a dose of clap to screw that little black bitch."

Dorothy suddenly ran from the game into her house and bedroom where she cowered, crying into the pillow. She didn't understand all of it but what she did understand frightened her. She knew they meant her and the fervor in their voices, the smirk, the emotion scared her. She didn't go out of the house again that day.

Many memories like that stayed with her. No psychiatry could cast them out.

When she was a little older, she stood in a bus with her arms full of school books on the first day of school. She was on her way home. Suddenly a finger was shoved violently into the cut between the cheeks of her backside. She reacted wildly, swinging hard at the young white boy who had violated her.

He hollered, "Why you little black bitch, you ought to be glad I dirtied my finger on your plump black ass." He kneed her in the groin and left the bus.

Dorothy cried and cried. It did no good. She couldn't erase this and similar incidents from her memory.

In school she became fond of another young white

girl named Alexandra. They went to movies together and ate lunch together at school. One day Alexandra brought Dorothy home to the furniture store that her father owned.

Her father was pleasant and had one of his clerks make them milk and sandwiches.

Everything was fine until Alexandra's mother came into the store. "Who is this?" she asked coldly. Alexandra explained that it was her best girl friend.

Her mother said to her father, "I want to talk to you." There was menace in her voice.

The two whispered in a corner of the store, then Alexandra's father said gently to Dorothy, "I'm afraid my little girl has some chores to do and it might be better if you go now."

Dorothy said pleasant goodbyes to everyone. A week later Alexandra's parents had her transferred to another school. Dorothy didn't quite put the pieces together until several years later when she met Alexandra at a party and it was all explained to her in detail.

Such incidents affected her entire perspective in later life. She told me, "I bathed in the glorious reviews of 'Carmen Jones.' I felt I had made a name for myself, made an imprint on my society. And then I read a review that had one line, a half line, 'Sometimes she threw around obvious sex.' It destroyed me. All the other compliments meant nothing. It was unfair. They disliked me. I was torn and crushed. So it was always. If one person in a thousand criticized me while all the others cheered, I didn't hear the cheers."

One time Dorothy was in a market buying bread and milk for the house. She was about twelve years old. She was standing in a line on the way to the cashier's desk and she felt a hand going into the slit in her wrap-around dress.

She turned quickly and a young white punk of six-teen or so smiled at her. She stamped on his foot and he yelled.

"Hey," the market manager shouted, "what's going on here?"

The punk said, "She stepped on my foot."

"Tell him why," Dorothy said, all flushed with anger.

"I don't know why," he said innocently.

She was so mad she stamped on his foot again.

He howled, and with that, the manager shoved Dorothy and said, "Don't ever come into this store again. You're a troublemaker." Dorothy tried to explain but got pushed out.

Dorothy was the girl who didn't have a daddy. That set her off from the other youngsters. When the kids would jibe her about it, she'd tell them her father was a very important man in the East. It didn't impress anyone.

Because she was brought up in a colored neighborhood, she didn't quite get the significance of the word "nigger" until she was older. It happened one day in the school auditorium. Two teachers were talking. One teacher ended up the conversation by saying, "The niggers will never give up until they own the country."

Dorothy wondered how the teacher could come to such a conclusion. She never expected the black people to own the country. She was satisfied if the whites would just let her alone.

Though clean and seemingly set apart from the tawdriness of Watts, Dorothy saw it all and if it didn't touch her physical self, there were imprints left. There were the drunks, white and black. In any poor neighborhood where the necessities are hard to find and the luxuries are non-existent, there is an excess of alcoholism.

Men lay in alleys or right out on the sidewalk, grim reminders of broken dreams. When they lay flat like that they bothered no one, but between the first drunk and the gutter, they were pesky and often dangerous.

Once a mean drunk tried to force a slug of red wine down Dorothy's throat. She fought like a tiger. When it spilled, he cuffed her. Another drunk came to her rescue and the two fought it out, much to her horror.

They both fell to the pavement, wrestling in the dirt until a policeman came and broke it up. He only pushed them on their way. He didn't arrest them. If every drunk in Watts were arrested, the jail would be full.

Dorothy stayed until it was all over. There was a horrible fascination to it all. When she told her mother about it, Ruby shrugged. That wasn't very important news and it was plain that nothing had happened to Dorothy.

Stepping over and being thrown into contact with these men---and women, we might add—was probably responsible for Dorothy's distaste for drink through many years. That is, until the forces and pressures forced her to pills and the bottle.

Even then she wouldn't drink in public. Even when things were the very worst, she'd drink behind closed doors.

As a child she loved the fire engines clanging to a fire. The firemen would wave to her, especially Thomas and William, two brothers who lived in the next block. She envied the fact that they were men. In those days, she felt if she were a fireman, she'd be eternally happy.

Often she'd run for blocks after the engines and if she could get to the destination, she'd stay until every spark was out.

Ruby had one driving ambition—that her children should never be domestics. She didn't know how to insure against it, however.

Her preacher suggested that the children enroll in some kind of school so they could learn a profession. Ruby almost automatically went to a dancing school.

Dorothy was fascinated with the dancing shoes and when Ruby bought her a pair, she was full of joy. It took only the enrollment of the girls into the dance school to give Ruby all sorts of ideas. The first step was to find another girl. Because of the popularity of the Andrew Sisters, girl trios were in demand. Ruby hired Etta Jones to become the third "Dandridge Sister" and formed a singing group called—what else?—The Dandridge Sisters. The next step was to enter a contest at radio station KNX, Los Angeles.

Then Ruby thought up a gimmick. She had them imitate the Andrews Sisters. They were the only Negro singers in the contest and they won first place.

Later, a circus hired the act for six months and took them to Hawaii. Dorothy was fourteen. It was a big adventure, the glorious beginning. She had stuck her toes in the water and found it refreshing.

She was on her own except for her "aunt," the group's accompanist who had been with the family since the Wonder Children days and who was to exert more and more influence on the children as time went by.

At this time, Ruby Dandridge was beginning a career of her own as a movie and radio comedienne and remained in Hollywood. She is still remembered for her long run as Oriole, co-starring with Hattie McDaniel on the Beulah radio show and latter as Judy Canova's pal on her show.

Once in Hawaii, Dorothy became friendly with a Hawaiian boy who was going to dramatic school. Dorothy enrolled, too, always convinced that knowledge was king. She felt study would give her advantages and she liked to act. All her life she took lessons, a trait inherited from her mother.

The "aunt" was in charge of the troupe and a strict disciplinarian. She influenced her relationship with men and restricted her movements and thinking.

By this time, however, Dorothy was old enough

now to sneak away when the situation demanded it. Dorothy never masked the fact that she hated the "aunt." In later years, she became quite violent when she spoke of her. "She was a superstitious old bat. She was often brutal and always threatening. She was jealous of me, too. She wanted the credit for making me successful, but on the other hand, she hated to see me succeed. I was always a target for her. She did everything she could to destroy me. It made it hard for me to cope with society later on."

In Hawaii, Dorothy took an interest in boys for the first time. It was the first indication that Dorothy's beauty was a powerful magnet. She developed more confidence and that was enough to make a good act a better one.

Talent agent Joe Glaser met the Dandridge Sisters and had no trouble selling them to Warner Brothers for a movie called "Going Places." It starred Dick Powell and Maxine Sullivan. His client Louis Armstrong was featured.

The audience liked them, and their act came to the attention of the MGM Shorts Department. Musical shorts were in vogue then. They did three shorts for MGM, all of them well received.

When they made "Going Places," everyone around the set made a big fuss over Dorothy. On another MGM short, "Snow Gets In Your Eyes," they sang "Harlem Yodel."

Joe Glaser liked her. He thought with some patient handling something could happen with her. So when she was fifteen, Joe took over and she was on the verge of show business' "big time."

Joe booked the Dandridge Sisters into the famous Cotton Club in Harlem. Duke Ellington saw the girls and booked them for radio and stage shows. Cab Calloway liked them, too, and had them sing with his band.

Dorothy, at seventeen, was beautiful and talented.

The girls had twelve boxes full of press clippings. They had the feel of success. And it was the beginning of Dorothy's urge to marry. You may say that every young single girl feels like that, but not like Dorothy. She needed someone she could love and trust, to rely on and protect her. She was afraid—afraid of some nameless thing.

When the girls were booked on a European tour that included the London Palladium (In London, an act had not "arrived" until it played the Palladium) and other dates throughout much of Europe, Dorothy dreamed of marrying some Italian count or English duke and living happily every after on the continent. The tour was interrupted by World War II and Dorothy met no romantic counts or dukes, just grimy privates in need of a kind word and a bath. The first she was able to give them.

Just after the girls began recording with Jimmy Lunceford, Etta Jones, who was then twenty-one, came home one night and quietly announced that she was getting married and quitting show business.

She had accomplished what Dorothy couldn't. She had found herself a husband. It was a happy time for Etta and a sad one for Dorothy. For one thing, they needed Etta in the act and, for another, Dorothy saw her friend do what she wanted to do most of all in the world—get married. Fortunately, Etta's "quitting" of show business did not take. She reached national prominence as a jazz singer in the late 1950s with (especially), "Don't Go To Strangers." She has continued to record and has something of a very loyal jazz cult following, and was nominated for a Grammy Award in 1998 for Best Jazz Album.

The Dandridge Sisters had just recorded two happy, wacky songs, "Red Wagon" and "Minnie The Moocher." Dorothy mused that she was lucky they had already done the happy songs because it would be hard for her to get "up" enough after the blow of Etta leaving the act.

The girls tossed a big party for Etta, and Dorothy's escort at the party was Harold Nicholas. Later he told her he was particularly taken by her because she had a chaperone. He didn't know girls actually had chaperones anymore. Had he been smart, he would have run, not walked, to the nearest exit. He should have known a girl who had a chaperone was too prim for a Broadway cynic like himself.

Dorothy had met Harold when she was at the Cotton Club. He was half of the Nicholas Brothers dance act. When she was there he noticed she turned down all dates. She was almost a freak to him, but a lovely freak. He had spent most of his adult years chasing girls and catching a lot of them. Dorothy wouldn't be caught. She was above such things.

If Harold hadn't been an idealist, he would have run from such unreality, but he was, and he asked Dorothy to marry him—even before they exchanged their first kiss.

The trio had broken up and Dorothy, as they say, was between engagements. She had nothing to think about but Harold and marriage. Still, she made him wait a bit.

Etta married, Vivian decided to do a solo act, and that left Dorothy to fend for herself. Right about this time, a legitimate revue titled "Meet The People" was in rehearsal. It satirized the news of the day in sketches and music. Dorothy took a part in it which required a solo song, some group work and sketches. It was a black and white cast. Harold Nicholas auditioned for it too but he wasn't hired.

It was the right show for Dorothy at this time. It explored all her talents and because there was no regard to ethnic background, she felt at ease. It turned out to be even better than she had hoped when the featured singer, Virginia O'Brien, became ill and Dorothy took over for her.

Virginia O'Brien was famous at that time for her dead-pan style. Dorothy couldn't imitate her but she got by and was particularly good in the sketches.

The reviewers were kind to her. She was proud of herself. It was a Federal Theater project and it received a great deal of attention. Dorothy was in what amounted to a hit show.

Then it was announced that MGM would make a movie of "Meet The People." By this time Dorothy knew a lot of influential people in the business including some of the brass at MGM where she had done shorts. She used every bit of leverage she could to get into the picture.

But this time her color tripped her up. It was explained to her rationally and diplomatically that the picture was going to be made with an all-white cast. One of the MGM executives told her, "The South isn't ready for colored actors. The picture would get shut out of a lot of key spots if it were made like the play. "I'm afraid there's no place for sentiment in this business," he told her. "We'd like to use more of the people from the play, but it just can't be done."

Dorothy cried bitter tears the first time that the color line erased her from the box. But "Meet The People" gave Dorothy a leg up for other things. She had proven that she could hold an audience from the stage.

In 1942 Duke Ellington asked her to appear in his musical show, "Jump For Joy." Herb Jeffries and Ivy Anderson were also in the musical.

She sang, "I Got It Bad And That Ain't Good."

With all this show business activity, she was the same old Dorothy. She went to the movies with Harold, but otherwise she didn't date. With all her sophistication in other areas, when it came to romance, Dorothy was a little girl.

She seldom went to parties and when she did, she drank Seven-Up. It was a real contrast to her bad years, during her marriage to Jack Dennison, when she'd sit

Dorothy with her bridegroom, Harold Nicholas, soon after their marriage in 1942. She was a virgin and the wedding night was a disaster. While she liked the idea of being married, keeping house and so forth, in the beginning she didn't understand why sex had to be a part of marriage.

She was incredibly innocent for having been in show business since the age of three. However, she was a lady and that appealed greatly to Harold who enjoyed having a lady for a wife but never for a moment gave up chasing other women. When the baby was born he tired of being married.

alone and consume a bottle of gin.

Harold noticed that she didn't smoke or drink anything—not even coffee—and if any conversation started that appeared to be headed for sex or four-letter words, she'd back off. Some show folks gave her the tag of "The Lady." She secretly liked that. Harold also loved her lady quality.

Harold Nicholas, with his brother, signed an MGM contract. He was in a financial position to marry. And on November 2, 1942, the marriage ceremony was performed. Harold was a peppery fellow, and an enthusiastic member of show business. If opposites attract, it should have been a perfect marriage. She was shy, quiet, respectable. He was noisy, extroverted and wild. He was a playboy who loved playing. She was satisfied to stay home, putter about the house and live a normal, quiet life.

Yet they had something going that led them into marriage. Harold wanted to marry a beautiful girl, a virgin with class. Dottie thought getting married was the right thing to do when you reach twenty and that Harold was Mr. Right. He respected her, was very successful, and he said he loved her.

The truth of the matter was, not only did Dorothy know virtually nothing about sex, she was terribly frightened and had never actually considered the facts of intimacy.

Certainly her fear was based in part on the horrible aftermath of a date she had when she was sixteen. We might add here, "sixteen and never been kissed." That's the kind of environment she came from. It was when she was living with her "aunt" in Los Angeles. Her mother, Ruby, was a dedicated actress and as head of the family was working much of the time, so the responsibility of raising Dorothy was left greatly to the stern "aunt."

"I'm going to the movies," Dorothy said. And her aunt gave her the usual warning, "Don't be late."

Ruby Dandridge as "Oriole," the character she played on the popular *Beulah* radio show of the 1940s and on television in the early 1950s in which she co-starred with Hattie McDaniel. She created her own niche in Hollywood and later played Judy Canova's friend on her television series.

Her date was a young clerk from the neighborhood whom she had gone to the movies with before. He was a shy lad who loved Dorothy, but from afar.

They misjudged the starting time of the picture and got in about the middle. It was a mystery film and Dorothy loved mysteries. So they saw the end of the film and then the whole film again. They were last out of the theater.

"It's so late," Dorothy said fearfully. She had lost track of all time. She was worried about the reaction of her aunt who was very strict.

They wasted more time while they stood on the sidewalk trying to find a good excuse Dorothy thought the woman would believe for their being so tardy. Then the time came when Dorothy had to face the reality of her situation. She shook her date's hand in a good night gesture and walked into the house full of foreboding.

Her aunt stood with hands on hips, lips tight, a terrifying sight.

"All right," she said, "where were you?"

Dorothy went into a long explanation and was so frightened she told the truth without any excuses. Her aunt didn't believe a word of it. "Now," she said slowly, "where were you?"

Dorothy began repeating the same excuse. Her aunt cut her short. She said wickedly, "Did you go to bed with him?"

Dorothy felt faint. She only shook her head in mute terror. "You did," her aunt insisted. "I have the feeling in my bones. I know you did. I just know it." She advanced on Dorothy. Though for what purpose other than a slap on the face, Dorothy had no idea. She would never have guessed why.

It was late at night and the world was quiet except for the walls of the old house creaking as it settled. Dorothy's voice sounded extra loud as she said, "Honest. We only stayed late in the theater. Why," she added, "he didn't even hold my hand."

But her aunt had the feeling in her bones. "We'll soon see," she said mysteriously. She advanced further on Dorothy. Dorothy retreated to the wall and then stood there, palms flattened against the peeled paint.

She remembered scenes like this in a movie but it was a man advancing. She pleaded again, "You can call Billy. He'll tell you. We did nothing wrong."

"I don't have to call Billy," her aunt said with a crooked smile. "I have my own way of finding out."

Dorothy thought, What in the world is she talking about? How can she find out? She thought maybe her aunt knew someone who had been to the movie and would check on her. She certainly wasn't ready for her aunt's own particular method of detection.

"We'll soon find out," her aunt said, "whether you're telling the truth. Which I doubt. Which I doubt very much. Take off your clothes."

Dorothy flinched. That she couldn't do. Her aunt knew she was shy about taking off her clothes in front of anyone.

So that was to be her punishment. She couldn't do it. "I can't," she just whispered.

"You can't," her aunt repeated. She walked up to Dorothy, with one hand behind Dorothy, one in front and with a synchronized dual motion pulled down the zipper and the dress at the same time.

This time she shrieked, "Take off your clothes!"

Dorothy began to sob and buried her face in her hands. Her aunt pulled down her half-slip with such fury she ripped it, and in the Dandridge household, it wasn't normal that good clothes were ripped. There was no surplus money.

Standing there in bra and panties, Dorothy felt so ashamed she couldn't look at her aunt.

"Follow me," her aunt ordered.

She followed dumbly into the bedroom.

"Get on the bed," her aunt pointed.

For a split second Dorothy felt the punishment was over. She would go to bed in bra and panties and that would be it. That was the furthest from what was in store. She sat on the bed.

"Take off your panties," her aunt thundered.

Dorothy couldn't believe her ears. No one had ever seen her private parts since she was a child. That was sacred.

"Well," her aunt shouted.

Dorothy was numb. She couldn't have moved even if she had wanted to. Her aunt must have gone crazy. The room was well lit. Even in the dark she wouldn't have taken them off. But not in the glaring light .

She put her hands protectively across her stomach. "No," she said firmly. It was the first time she had ever answered her aunt in that decisive tone of voice.

Her aunt was on her like a tiger. Dorothy fought back. They struggled and rolled together on the bed like whirlwinds. They both were strong. But the cotton panties were no match for Dorothy's aunt. They ripped off in tatters leaving her only with her bra, perspired and humiliated.

It was nothing to what was coming. Auntie managed to sit on Dorothy's back while she wrestled her face down to the bed. With one hand she held Dorothy's face to the bed. Then with the other she worked her fingers into Dorothy's behind and then down into her vagina. Dorothy screamed in terror. The finger groped and pulled until her aunt was satisfied.

She struggled, screaming "Stop it! Stop it!" But her aunt didn't stop until she was satisfied. Then she got off Dorothy and said, "All right, you're still a virgin. But then maybe it's because he didn't put it in all the way."

"What are you talking about?" Dorothy sobbed. Her crotch hurt and she had two bad scratches on her lower stomach. "What?" she screamed.

Her aunt looked smug. "Go to sleep," she ordered. "Next time you'll get home when you should."

Dorothy cried herself to sleep.

Scenes of degradation like this punctured Dorothy's childhood. They piled one on the other until her wedding night. She entered into marriage with Harold Nicholas a virgin. He never questioned it for a moment. He wanted her to be a virgin.

Now it was the wedding night and the slim, good-looking man looked with approval at his bride. There she was at twenty years of age one of the world's most beautiful women—and untouched.

And he was proud of her. Who wouldn't be?

And she stood in her bridal gown in this Los Angeles hotel room knowing this was it. Soon she would go to bed with her husband. Not right this minute—soon. That was the word that would let her think—soon.

He was speaking but she wasn't listening. He was laughing so she laughed. Maybe he had been telling a joke. She had to laugh. She wished it was tomorrow. If only twenty-four hours would pass without her knowing it.

God, what a cliche situation—a honeymoon night. After all, she was in show business. She had been exposed to sex all her life. Sex and talk of sex. But it had never touched her. Why was she so frightened? She loved Harold. Yet why did sex have to go with love? After all, she and Harold had been happy without sex all this time. Why did sex have to enter into it now?

She looked at Harold. He was smoking a cigarette. His shoes were off. He was relaxed. She knew about Harold. He had been a swinger. She knew that. He had slept with many girls. He had never been hypocritical about it. He was satisfied for her to be a virgin, but he had despoiled many a girl. She even knew some of them. A couple were famous movie actresses.

She wasn't jealous. That's the way men were. Why

couldn't she be natural—accept sex as a human desire without embarrassment or fear? But she couldn't. Her heart was palpitating and her knees felt weak. She'd have to snap out of it. She couldn't go to bed with Harold the first time like this.

He had picked up a paper and was talking about a film at the studio that he had a chance of getting into.

She smiled. She didn't trust her voice. She puttered and hung up her clothes. It was long after midnight. The time had almost come. She felt a little ill and wondered if there were any pills in the bag her aunt had packed that would help. She went through her suitcase but there were only aspirins.

"Honey, let's go to bed," Harold said loudly. So loudly she felt it would rock the bathroom door.

"Yes, dear," she was able to say. She tried not to think. She saw the shower and decided that would give her precious extra minutes. Also Harold would hear the shower and understand it would take a little more time for her to get ready.

She took a long time to get the water just right. She thought as she stood there nude and shivering, "Maybe I never should have gotten married. Maybe there are certain girls who aren't fit for marriage." But now it was too late.

The warm water felt good on her skin. She stayed there until Harold shouted, "Okay, you're clean enough. Come on to bed."

She could tell by his voice he was already in bed. She stopped the shower and dried herself off. She sprayed herself with a new perfume that had been a wedding present from a girl friend.

It smelled good and for a moment it seemed to whisk away the fears. She donned her flimsy powder blue negligee and looked in the mirror.

There was no sign of nerves. She looked perfectly all right. There were blue silk panties that went with the negligee. Should she wear them too? She hesitated for some time and then donned them.

She walked toward the door and opened it. Now she knew about the last walk of prisoners to the electric chair.

The room was dark except for light coming in through a window. Harold snapped his fingers and laughingly said, "Just follow the sound of love."

"Okay," she said. Her voice sounded crackly to her.

She walked to the bed and then said something stupid. "Should I get in?"

He laughed. "Sure," he said. "We paid for the room. The bed goes with it."

She got into bed carefully, being extra conscious of his being there and staying on her side of the bed.

"Come to big daddy," he said, and pulled her gently to him.

She couldn't tell him she was sick to her stomach. She would look foolish. He had his arms around her and she was pressed to him. He was telling her how much he loved her.

She managed to squeeze it out, "I love you, too."

He hugged her. She closed her eyes and prayed she could get through the next few minutes without making an ass of herself. His hands were now skirting lightly over her whole body. She tried not to breathe. It was a mistake. He took the long out-breath to be passion.

"Take off your nightie," he said.

When she didn't move immediately, he helped her off with it. He scooted out of his pajamas. They were nude in each other's arms. This was a first for her. This was the moment she had been dreading all these years. What was wrong with her? Why wasn't she like other girls? She felt like crying.

Harold's hands were exploring her. She was embarrassed and ill. She remembered that night with her aunt. It wasn't a lot different.

He was kissing her all over. She tried not to think

and just accept it. This was part of marriage.

Between kisses he told her of his great love for her. His voice barely penetrated. She felt as if she had turned to stone.

Poor Harold, she thought. He didn't know what he was getting. She'd just have to stand it. The moment was here. Right now. She tried to hold her breath again.

"Your legs, darling," he said.

At first she didn't know what he was driving at. Then when his fingers dug into her thighs and he pulled, she knew she had missed her cue. She opened her legs wide, very wide.

"Good girl," he said. He climbed on top of her and prepared to enter. She was tight—too tight. He grunted.

It hurt and she said without meaning to, "Don't."

Somehow his laugh after all her tension upset her. "Don't," she shouted and she pushed him off.

She sat up in bed.

"What the hell's wrong?" he screamed. "You want it, don't you?"

"No." She said it forcefully.

"Well, I'll be a sonofabitch," he said. "What the hell do you think marriage is all about? Dating and presents? Hell no. It's intimacy. Without it, sister, down the drain. Without sex, marriage is a barrel of problems—troubles." He changed his tone. "Come on, honey." He pulled her toward him. "You'll get used to it. It won't hurt. I'll be very gentle."

"No," she said determinedly. "I don't want to. I don't feel like it."

There was complete silence for a few moments.

"We'll see about that," he said grimly. He pulled her to him and wrestled her flat on her back. She struggled silently.

"We're going to have fun, baby," he said. "I'm here to guarantee it."

The tap dancing Nicholas Brothers. Dorothy Dandridge got a crush on Harold (left) when she was only fifteen and the Dandridge Sisters were on the bill with the Nicholas Brothers at the Copa nightclub in New York. Seven years later they were married but the relationship turned out to be a disaster.

Dorothy Dandridge's mother on her steel drum s with her Island Band. Ruby, who had show business aspirations from the beginning, became moderately successful in both her music and acting careers. As a matter of fact, she was so occupied with her own career that she allowed the woman Dorothy

referred to as her "aunt" to tour with the Dandridge Sisters. Later Dorothy told
Earl Mills that she hated the woman and described several acts of abuse she'd
suffered at the hands of her "aunt." At least one of them could account for
Dorothy's fear of sex at the time she married.

Years later, in this scene from a film with Stuart Whitman, originally entitled *The Decks Ran* Red (released as *Infamy At Sea*) Dorothy was able to call on memories of her wedding night when she was raped by her impatient husband, Harold Nicholas, to give a bitterly convincing performance.

CHAPTER FIVE

It's not easy to commit rape—the logistics are against it. But that's what Harold had to do. Dorothy was pinned down but her legs were glued together. All the forced kisses from her husband accomplished nothing. It made her fight harder.

He was angry now. He appealed for justice. "You're my wife. What the hell did you think being a wife would be?"

She fought silently. All she knew was that she wasn't ready for conjugal bliss. She resented it and it frightened her. Still she was obligated. She knew that. But her conscience wasn't enough to make her submit.

Harold stopped wrestling for a moment to get some air. He was breathing furiously.

She lay there panting. She felt scratches smarting and bruises hurting. But she was determined she wouldn't cry.

Then a strange thing happened. Harold got off her. He lay beside her. "What am I doing?" He asked himself the question out loud. "I must be crazy. You don't want me. Fine. It's your privilege. We'll get an annulment. That's all. Why fight?"

Dorothy felt sorry for him. It wasn't Harold. He

had nothing to do with it. It was the whole idea. It was repugnant to her. And frightening.

Harold lay next to her in silence. She wondered if he would go to sleep. That would be so wonderful. She felt in the morning she'd be able to think and handle all this. Right now it was too much.

"Good night," he said pleasantly.

"Good night," she responded.

She knew she was wrong—very wrong. She knew she was being childish. But could she submit to sexual intercourse? It seemed horrifying. She lay awake for hours until she heard Harold's measured breathing.

She didn't want a divorce, an annulment. She loved Harold. She needed a man even if it was just to get away from her aunt. If only sex didn't have to go with it, how perfect it would be.

She tried to imagine the sex act from start to finish. It wasn't so terrible, she told herself. She could stand it. She rehearsed how she would make herself numb and blot out all thoughts. She had done this during other crises. It wasn't hard.

She must not get an annulment. It would spoil everything. She wanted to be married.

What to do? She put her hand on Harold's chest. He awoke from a deep sleep. "What?" he asked.

"I'm sorry," she said. "I'm really sorry."

"Oh?"

"Just try and understand. I've had a different kind of life. But I'm willing to try again. Be patient." She kissed him.

This time the sexual act was accomplished. Afterward Dorothy had no recollection of it. She was successful in blotting everything out.

That's the way their marriage started. It was doomed from the start.

If there were no sex in the marriage, Dorothy would have been the happiest married woman in America. She liked all the other aspects of marriage.

In 1942, Duke Ellington asked Dorothy to appear in his new musical show, "Jump For Joy" which also starred Herb Jeffries (above, with Dorothy) and Ivy Anderson. She sang "I Got It Bad And That Ain't Good." When she left the show she married Harold Nicholas, the man she'd had a crush on for years.

She adored keeping a house clean and livable, cooking, waiting for Harold to come home each night (it was often a long wait) and mixing with all the other young married women. She gave up show business, forever she thought.

She worried about how Harold was accepting her inexperience in bed. But she never talked about it to him. It was a subject that embarrassed her.

Harold gave her all the money she needed and she was happy with him. Yet she worried that he wasn't happy with her.

Actually, he was happy. He had a house, a roost for himself and still he swung around town just as he always had. If Dorothy wasn't the greatest in bed, it didn't matter. There were others.

He was proud of her and her beauty. He liked to be seen with her. She dressed beautifully and they had a lot of status in the Negro community.

When she became pregnant, both thought the child would bring them even closer together. Dorothy became an even better wife and the pregnancy gave her an excuse to cut down on their sexual relations.

It still didn't bother Harold because he was often away on tour or location and there were plenty of girls, black and white, for his fun and games.

Dorothy had traveled with her husband to Europe before her pregnancy, but now she stayed home and prepared for the baby.

Because Harold was away much of the time, she enrolled in the Actor's Lab in Hollywood. This gave her a new insight into the Negro question. At the lab color meant nothing and she could play any part.

It awakened her to what was going on outside her classes. For the first time she decided she'd never take for granted any put-down of the Negro. She'd fight for human dignity.

She became aware that it was a mistake to put down all whites as so many of her Negro friends did.

There must be a joint fight for equality. It was a big subject for her and one that would haunt her all her life.

Her marriage collapsed with the first sign that daughter Harolyn (called Lynn) had suffered some kind of brain damage.

In the beginning friends and doctors told her some children were slower than others in learning to walk and speak.

When these first suspicions arose as to the mental normalcy of the child, Harold was in Europe. When he came back to a distraught Dorothy, he wasn't too upset over it. That made Dorothy even more distraught. Now all her waking hours were devoted to the child and Harold was forgotten. Bored with it all, he left again for Europe. His comment was that a Negro was an equal in Europe and the Europeans were more civilized. He was also successful there.

Dorothy took the baby from one doctor to another begging for hope which they could not give her. It was now apparent that the child was retarded. Tests were made, specialists called in and the future for Lynn as a normal young lady appeared bleak.

Dorothy was broken-hearted. She blamed herself. She blamed Harold. She blamed the doctor who delivered her. She blamed God. But it did no good. These were the facts.

Dorothy's long impassioned letters to Harold about the child's retardation brought only silence. He was sorry but he didn't want his life, or for that matter Dorothy's, to suffer because of it. He was a fatalist and a realist.

He indicated in a short letter to her that he liked Paris and he was going to live there. He stopped sending her money. His letter was apologetic but the facts were clear. She could expect no more help from him.

Her funds were just about gone. She had a mentally retarded child, no career and no husband. She'd question herself often as she cried herself to sleep. How did it happen? How?

Things became worse. Her health broke down. She was destitute. Only her family stuck by her.

She carried a picture of herself with Lynn when the child was a year old. Lynn was beautiful and the child looked normal. Dorothy showed the picture to everyone. This was the dream. This was how it could have been.

When she saw little girls on the street, she'd stop and talk to them. Then she'd cry.

The final verdict was in. Harolyn would always have the mentality of a four-year-old.

Dorothy would vacillate between despair and hope. She said she'd never give up. She'd spend days looking at medical books and magazines, suddenly finding a hope, pursuing it and then having it dashed once more.

One night her aunt burst into Dorothy's house and insisted Dorothy put Lynn in an asylum. Dorothy was aghast at such a thought. In the end, of course, it had to be done. But in the meantime, Dorothy convinced her aunt that maybe she could help the child. Her aunt liked the idea.

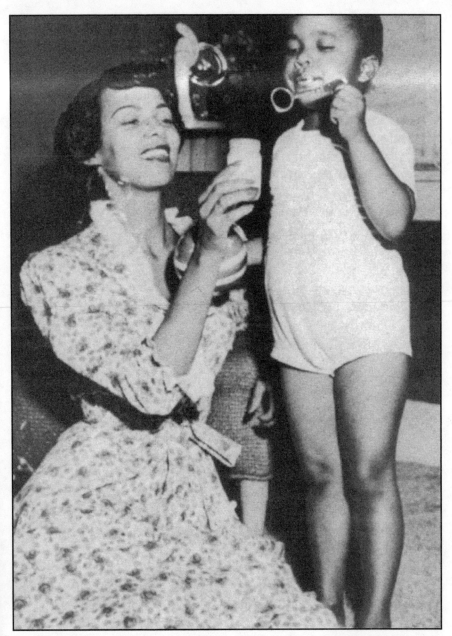

Soon after Dorothy's divorce, her "aunt" who was still living with Ruby burst into her house one night and insisted she put Harolyn into an "asylum" which, in the end, had to be done. Meanwhile Dorothy talked the Aunt into looking after the child, so she could find work. The aunt agreed.

Dorothy in a still photograph from *Tarzan's Peril*. She had not worked for some years, during her marriage to Harold Nicholas, when she made the film for Sol Lesser, a low budget affair in which starred her as a "jungle princess" opposite Lex Barker as Tarzan. Yet, she was impressive in the film.

CHAPTER SIX

With Harolyn at her aunt's house, Dorothy could take stock of herself. If she continued on this way, she'd be no good to herself or anyone else. Her life would be over. She'd have to find work again. Yet she hadn't worked in so long, she was rusty. She wasn't even sure she had a voice left.

Fate took a hand. She was shopping in a market and a young man greeted her. Phil Moore. He was a music arranger and composer who had arranged songs for the Dandridge Sisters when they were working for Cab Calloway at the Cotton Club in New York.

They walked and Dorothy poured out her whole story. It was a long and heartbreaking one.

Phil had always liked Dorothy—romantically—and he offered to help. He thought if he coached her she could work up a solo act and play the night clubs.

Dorothy was willing to try.

Phil was talented and sincere. He had worked for Lena Horne, done big band arrangements for Harry James and others. And because of his talent and the fact that he was well-liked, he was able to live in an all-white neighborhood above the Sunset Strip—an unheard of occurrence in those days.

There was another apartment available in Phil's building at the time, and he convinced Dorothy that she should take it. When she mentioned money, he waved her protests aside. He was willing to help until she could start making money again. Phil was sure it would only be a matter of time until Dorothy would be important once more.

His confidence in her, her need for success and love, led to their having a love affair.

This was all different for Dorothy. She was accustomed to being married and not working. Now she was adrift again in the world of show business. Dorothy felt lost and inadequate. She was reluctant to sing because she was afraid, but she felt she had to. Phil was good to her and she felt she couldn't let him down.

Desi Arnaz was playing the Mocambo at that time with a small band. His girl singer became ill and Phil begged Desi to let Dorothy try for the spot.

Desi agreed and Dorothy worked for a few days, not sure of herself, but trying for all she was worth. Some agents saw her and signed her to open in a small club in Seattle.

Dorothy knew her faults. She had no poise. She was frightened, not sure and lost. The Seattle club canceled her stay.

Phil did all he could to cheer Dorothy up. He still felt that time would work for her. He tried doubly hard to find her work.

Phil's friend, Sol Lesser, was producing *Tarzan's Peril*. Lex Barker was Tarzan and the script called for a beautiful jungle princess to be his mate. Phil persuaded Dorothy to test for the role. She did and was signed.

She was fine in a role that made few demands. As a result of the film, Columbia Pictures cast her in a movie about the Harlem Globetrotters. She was to be the girl friend of a famous Negro athlete. She did the part and was adequate in the role.

It was soon after that I went to a Sunday musicale

at Phil Moore's apartment and met Dorothy Dandridge
for the first time. It was April 1951.

I talked to Dorothy. There was no way then of
priming that well of emotional fervor that was camou-
flaged by her serenity. Our conversation was antisep-
tic—polite, formal. It was no indication of the excite-
ments to come.

"Will you sing for me some time?" I asked.

"Some time," she responded quietly. It was a toss-
up as to whether she ever would.

Every Sunday there was a musicale. I was there
and so was Dorothy. It seemed she became more beautiful each week. Being practical minded, I thought if I
took such pleasure out of just looking at her, millions of
other men would.

A talent is a jigsaw puzzle. A talent must have it
all—looks, talent, magnetism, poise, ambition, loyalty,
need. I desperately wanted her to have all the crazy
cardboard pieces so she could be complete. She had
them.

Then came that magic evening. Phil said casually
that Dorothy would sing for me.

Her first song was "A Woman's Prerogative." Phil
accompanied her. It was no casual performance. She
poured herself into the melody and caressed the words.

Phil explained that Dorothy preferred to sing bal-
lads. I studied her every move and listened intently to
every sound. Something disturbed me. Midway
through the number I knew what it was. She came to
life when she sang "A Woman's Prerogative," and she
created no interest when she sang serious, tragic bal-
lads, which she loved doing.

She sang in her favorite costume of skirt and
sweater. She wore no shoes. Yet her face and manner
were full of elegance. The two didn't mesh.

In my mind's eye, I saw her in a beautiful long
gown with all the formal accessories as the setting for
her loveliness. She was born to be adored, put on a

pedestal.

That's what was wrong. She should sing personality—light, happy and sophisticated love songs. She was a beautiful painting that needed a beautiful frame. How could I tell her without hurting her feelings? She told me she wanted to sing "Good For Nothing Joe." Talent is always sensitive to any criticism. I'd have to tread softly.

My trouble was I looked at her as a girl first born, a fault over-indulged in by idealists. For the moment, I wasn't aware of any past for Dorothy Dandridge. All she was and had been was standing there right now. She had never been a child, a teenager, had lovers, family, troubles, complications, disappointments or a past. For me, she had been born that minute.

But the truth was she had a tragic past. All of it could, with some discernment by the viewer, be seen on her face. I saw wholesome loveliness, personal magnetism, charm, warmth.

Dorothy and I had many long talks over the following months. I felt that she was a tremendous talent destined for great heights in the show world. I wanted to manage her career because I firmly believed in her talent and because I was already a little bit in love with her.

Dorothy at this time was in constant conflict with herself. She was ambitious and realized her need to get ahead in the only profession that she knew. She was still terribly not sure of herself, her talent and abilities.

Dorothy finally convinced herself that she could make it; more important that she had to. "I'm broke. Close to it, anyway. My career is at a standstill. My marriage has ended in divorce and I have a child to provide for. I must make a move."

Her first move came without any connection to my efforts. But it was a turning point for her. Suddenly a series of events, propelled by fate, caught her, Phil and myself in a whirlwind of activity.

In 1951 the Sunset Strip was pretty much at its glamorous height. It was long before the hippie made inroads on it. Those were the days when Ciro's and the Mocambo were two of the most important clubs in America for an entertainer.

The heavyset, cigar puffing Herman Hover ruled over Ciro's and small, dapper Charlie Morrison ran Mocambo. Either man by lifting a finger could make a performer into a star name.

Dorothy was destined to go unexpectedly into the Mocambo and overnight become a national celebrity.

Meanwhile, in the center of the Strip on a slight rise on Horn Avenue was the Club Gala, run by two brothers, Jim and Frank Dolan. It was an "in" spot frequented by many celebrities because of an entertainer named Johnny Walsh who later was to own his club on La Cienega Boulevard.

The Cafe Gala was then a hangout for many known homosexuals as well as celebrities who were straight. In those days, especially, and to a point even today, Hollywood gays and lesbians in the arts often led the way. Where they went, the important people followed.

That happened at the Cafe Gala both with the customers and often with talent where great entertainers broke in.

Walsh, with a sophisticated cynicism, was the darling of the Hollywood set but had been overworked for a long time. He insisted on having a vacation. So the owners talked to agents about a replacement.

Walsh had drawn the crowds and the owners didn't want to lose them. Independent agent Lou Irwin suggested Phil Moore with a trio. Phil had that flair for amusing and titillating the Hollywood crowd, and he was well known in Los Angeles.

Phil was approached and he said he'd like to bring in Dorothy Dandridge with his trio. They agreed after Jim Dolan met Dorothy.

You must understand that no one was more beautiful or sophisticated on the outside than Dorothy. But inside she was Jell-O, a quivering mass of insecurities and uncertainties.

Opening night, as a result of nerves, she lost most of her voice. She was so distraught when she stepped out on stage for the first time, Phil had to help her to the Steinway and she had to sit instead of stand.

She had worked with her sister as a team before and had appeared before the impersonal film cameras, but she feared facing a live audience alone.

She was petrified. Months later she admitted she remembered nothing about that opening night. Between shows she sat so frightened she couldn't speak.

Phil knew Dorothy's shortcomings and was prepared for them. He loosened her up with jokes and patter between numbers that required she talk back and forth with him. He got her to look at and focus on the audience. They felt no communication with her. Phil soon fixed that by coaching her all through the day so that at night she'd forget herself and concentrate on the audience.

After a few nights, Dick Williams, entertainment editor of the Los Angeles Mirror, came in. He sat fascinated with this lovely Negro singer. He sat through each show, every song, and didn't leave until the place closed. He came back every night. He was the first to be hypnotized by her.

A part of his review read, "It's on nights like last, with the rain splashing against the black windows and the candles on the big grand piano glowing steadily, that you could climb the hill above the Sunset Strip to hear Dorothy Dandridge."

This front page cover story for the Weekend Amusement Guide with five large photos became the first big break in Dorothy's career.

"Dorothy Dandridge gives everything to her songs. The satiny, sexy songstress has that starlight aura. She has beauty, an infectious good humor, sexy delivery and an extremely clever style. This is Dorothy Dandridge, the most exciting new sepia singer I've spotted.

"She leans there on the piano at the end of that room which has the feel of a Manhattan-style intimate supper club, eyes closed, lips parted, her hands thrown in front of her, the fringe of her white dress flying as she huskily intones, 'Got Harlem On My Mind,' 'Sweet Talk,' 'Buy, Buy, Buy For Baby,' and 'A Woman's Prerogative.'" Dorothy became the favorite of newsmen. They understood her honesty, her humanness.

All a cafe entertainer must have is rave reviews. Dorothy got them and the crowds followed. She was suddenly the talk of the town. The good notices and the crowds gave her the confidence she needed. Now she was the Dorothy Dandridge who had the opportunity to earn large sums as a club entertainer and picture star. She was on her way up.

I noticed Mocambo owner Charlie Morrison at the Gala a few times. He sat morosely at the back of the room through Dorothy's act and I knew what was coming—and it did.

Dorothy was asked to walk up Sunset Boulevard after her engagement at the Gala and open at the Mocambo. Of course, Phil and Dorothy were delighted.

Neither talked about it, but Phil Moore and Dorothy Dandridge had the town on its ear.

On the sixth night, Maurice Winnick, a British theatrical impresario, came to the Cafe Gala with Lou Irwin. He offered Dorothy an engagement in London at the Cafe de Paris. They accepted.

Yet there was a cloud over the triumph. Winnick put into words what everyone had been thinking—the people came to see and hear Dorothy Dandridge. Phil Moore was important, but secondary. There were long discussions over billing.

Dorothy had not played a club for several years when she ran into Phil Moore who had arranged songs for the Dandridge Sisters when they were working for Cab Calloway in New York. He convinced Desi Arnaz to use her for a few days at the Mocambo, then got them booked into the Cafe Gala, a club

which catered to gays and celebrities, never an unusual venue in Hollywood. They were an immediate hit, especially after Dick Williams of the Herald Examiner ran a photo spread on Dorothy and gave her a rave review. Some three decades later the Cafe Gala became Spago.

Phil Moore was an artist and his pride and ego were hurt by all of this. After all, his act alone, without Dorothy, had made hit records. He had spent many years working with Lena Horne. He was respected in the trade as a fine talent. Now he didn't want to be squeezed out. He fancied himself the brains, director of strategy of the combination. He fought to hold onto his position.

The two opened on July 9th in London and the billing read, "Dorothy Dandridge (very large) with Phil Moore (half as large)." It did not make Phil very happy.

The Cafe de Paris had a moving center stage so that Dorothy was always in front and Phil behind. The act also included seven white English musicians. White-wigged attendants escorted Dorothy down the stairs to the stage for her entrance.

Her gowns were beautiful but not lavish. She became subtle and sophisticated, fearing London crowds would expect an American entertainer to be overbearing, loud and forceful. She decided to play it easy and cool.

Reviews were glowing yet the wordage all went to Dorothy. There were long meetings while advertising was discussed. Phil had no complaints about money— Dorothy was happy with a fifty/fifty cut. But the British wanted more and more emphasis on Dorothy. Phil rebelled. Then Dorothy sensed an attempt by her associate to cut in on her lines on stage—grab more of the spotlight, try for more personal attention. They began to bicker and it burst into a loud argument at a London club.

Soon they apologized to each other, but the reconciliation was a cool one. Dorothy cried a lot and Phil lapsed into moody silences.

When the engagement was finished, they hardly spoke. Both knew it was the end of the road together.

When Dorothy returned to Los Angeles, she called

me to ask me to have dinner with her. I sensed what it would be about. She looked more beautiful than ever, even though obviously distraught over her break-up with Phil. She explained in detail why her business and personal relationship with Phil was at an end.

She wanted to remain his friend and made a big point of paying him for everything he had done—for arrangements and material. But she had grown up and she wanted a career of her own. It was in her eyes—finally there was ambition there.

She asked me to become her personal manager, and I agreed to. We were at last a team. She signed a contract on November 17, 1951, and we gradually became inseparable, with the exception of her married years to Jack Dennison.

Dorothy Dandridge at opening night at the Mocambo Club on the Sunset Strip. At the time the Mocambo and Ciro's were the happening clubs on the Strip. After her success at Cafe Gala, Mocambo owner Charlie Morrison (later Johnnie Ray's father in law) booked her into his club. She was sensational.

CHAPTER SEVEN

Now that I was about to help make Dorothy Dandridge become the big star she deserved to be, I wanted to know more about her. It was important to me.

She told me a little of her life. At first she wasn't very revealing. It was apparent she was bitter about white men who looked on a Negro girl as just a hot bed partner. She gave an example. When she was in London, a baron came to the stage entrance laden with flowers for her. On the long stem of one rose there hung a beautiful jade and gold charm bracelet. Dorothy couldn't help but respond to the baron's generosity since he visited her every night at the Cafe and always with a gift.

The baron was a fast car enthusiast, wealthy and handsome. He had just gotten over an international divorce and said he was depressed by possessive love during six years of unhappy marriage. Dorothy silently was determined not to be too possessive of this relationship, should it go anywhere.

The two dated several times and then the baron took her to his home. It covered several acres of ground on the outskirts of London. The great stone balustrades and a large stone bridge were very impressive to

Dorothy in contrast to the tiny wood frame house she was brought up in.

Dorothy also thought in typical feminine vein how wonderful it would be if the baron should propose marriage to her. She could see herself living high on the hog for the rest of her life.

The first eccentricity Dorothy noted upon entering the castle was that the servants—and there were many of them—were all midgets. The baron began the evening by being the perfect host. He was attentive and good humored. Dorothy was almost disarmed. She was always on her guard with white men. She told the rest of it this way:

"He insisted I drink some black wine his own winery had made. Since he sipped of it too, I felt safe in drinking it. I shouldn't have. I felt very sleepy soon after I drank it—not uncomfortable or dizzy, just sleepy.

"Then everything started. His retinue of midget servants came in and undressed him and then put him in what looked like a woman's nightie, very silky and very sheer. I tried to protest but I was too weak to move. It was all like a dream.

"He explained that he loved me and therefore he was going to pay me a lot of money to make love to him. Of course I protested. He didn't seem to listen but I watched while two girl midgets practiced every kind of perversion on him. He seemed unquenchable, never tiring.

"I found later that he had no intention of making love to me. His kick was having me watch while all this was happening to him.

"I think I sat there for several hours while male and female midgets romped over him performing every type of sexual exercise.

"When I gained my strength, I got up and insisted he take me back to the hotel. His midgets dressed him, he quietly took me back and I never saw him again. I wondered how many women had gone through this. There is just one postscript. I got a card from him in the States saying he was so taken by me he had added a Negro dwarf to his staff! I didn't know men could be like that."

Dorothy changed the subject to business. We both felt it was necessary to keep Phil Moore on in a musical capacity. He understood Dorothy's talent and could augment her artistry. He needed her and she needed him, but only in the background.

We later found a replacement to do her accompaniment. We needed Phil, a good pianist and arranger and composer and Dorothy was booked immediately into the Mocambo, this time with much more fanfare. It was a two-week engagement with owner Charlie Morrison sending out elaborate promotional brochures to customers reading, "Miss Dandridge is a volume of sex with the living impact of the Kinsey Report."

Three 9x14 photos of Dorothy dominated the brochure.

Life magazine lent impact to her opening with four pages devoted to her and called her, "The most beautiful Negro singer since Lena Horne."

This was the beginning of the upsurge that would make her an international star. Life continued to follow her career and in November, 1954, they used for the *first* time in Life's history a photo of a Negro on the cover.

Ebony Magazine, an influential publication for the black race, featured Dorothy on the cover and inside spoke in glowing terms about how proud the black race was of Dorothy. This made her very happy. Until this moment, she had heard that her black friends were disappointed in her. They accused her of going over to the white side and snobbishly turning her back on her black brothers. On the other hand, to many Caucasians, Dorothy was still a beautiful light-skinned Negro who could entertain them but most were edgy about letting her mix with them. The dilemma of being disliked by many in both worlds constantly worried Dorothy. She tried doing what she could to help dispel these prejudices. Soon she was to do what no Negro had ever done before—open at the Waldorf-Astoria in New York, live and work in a luxurious Missouri hotel and be invited to live in a large Miami Beach resort hotel—an amazing accomplishment at that time.

In December, 1951, she signed with a new agency, MCA, with me as her manager and friend, and with national publicity from Life, a very ambitious Dorothy became determined to become a big star. She was determined to make it on her own—no longer the child star of "The Wonder Children" or with sister Vivian and Etta Jones as "The Dandridge Sisters" touring all over the world.

Out of the limelight, Dorothy was as shy as ever. She kept exercising extensively to work off all her tensions. She was either under great tension or very calm, never in between.

With her new accompanist, Ernie Freeman, some new songs and some new glamorous gowns, Dottie left for her first MCA tour for Rochester, Buffalo, Toronto and Miami Beach. Both Dorothy and I always insisted that she live where she worked or close by if her engagement wasn't in a hotel.

Dorothy with fans at the London society club, Cafe de Paris. Maurice Winnick, a British theatrical impresario had stopped in at the Cafe Gala to catch Dorothy's act with Phil Moore. He was so impressed that he offered her the engagement. Her top billing there hurt Phil Moore's feelings.

With her career back on track thanks to Phil Moore and her performances at Cafe Gala and the Mocambo, Dorothy was no longer, as she'd put it shortly before, "broke, my career is at a standstill. My marriage has ended in divorce and I have a child to provide for." Now, she was able to relax a bit.

CHAPTER EIGHT

Dorothy was to contracted to open a new club in Miami Beach, Ciro's, along with Tony and Sally DeMarco and Larry Storch.

I was told point-blank by Joe Scully, the MCA representative in New York, that Negroes could not live in Miami Beach. There was a city ordinance that wouldn't permit it and it was strictly enforced. According to Joe, Negroes, and that meant Dorothy, were allowed in Miami Beach at night only if they worked there and had a work pass. They could not live in any Miami Beach hotel.

Dorothy was furious. She wanted to cancel out but I persuaded her not to. I said, "Let's see what we can do to minimize and fight prejudice." I talked to Sandy Scott, Ciro's owner, and he said, "I will help fight that ordinance. I'll see what can be done."

The fact is, there were restrictions on Negroes all over Florida and restaurants wouldn't serve them. I made reservations for Dorothy, her black pianist Ernie Freeman and myself at the Lord Calvert Hotel in the segregated ghetto, hoping to work out a change after we got there. We couldn't find another place to live.

Her dear friend, Nat "King" Cole, also had to live in the Miami ghetto when he worked in Miami Beach.

She was fit to be tied. Sandy Scott offered his Miami home and the loan of his car. Dorothy thought it unwise to stay at his home. He was a bachelor.

You can imagine the mood she was in. When opening night arrived, to add to Dorothy's angry mood was the fact there had been unexpected delays in construction and the club really wasn't ready for the opening. The main room was just about half ready but the kitchen was still unfinished and the staff not sufficiently rehearsed in view of the obstacles presented.

However, Scott was committed. The ad budget was as high as the entertainment budget. He had to open and hope everything would work out. It was impossible. Workmen were still tinkering while the overture sounded. Unfinished construction made it impossible for the waiters to give decent service. The food was slow coming out of the kitchen , and the customers waited, what seemed like to them, forever.

No one is harder to please than a hungry customer.

To further complicate the problems, none of the dressing rooms for the entertainers were ready. They had to change in the rest rooms. Larry Storch, who is usually one of the entertainment's steady performers, didn't get a laugh. He pulled out all the stops, but there was no reaction. The customers could only think of the lack of food, service and the noise. There were pots everywhere and a lousy sound system. Sally and Tony DeMarco followed and the act just laid there—no applause. Dorothy was reluctant to go out, but she did. No reaction at all. They all flopped and the customers still hadn't been fed. It was a shambles. It should teach all entrepreneurs something. An audience, whether for a film, play or musical, has to be happy and comfortable in order to enjoy entertainment. If they are hungry, cold, hot or in hard seats and can't see or hear— beware!

After that night, the owner decided to finish construction before reopening the club. That put Dorothy in a spot: A colored girl with no job in the segregated ghetto of Miami Beach.

But there was a bright spot. Despite Dorothy's poor showing at Ciro's, two hungry diners that night appreciated her. Nick Kelly and Nat Harris, who were associated with Monte Prosser in the operation of La Vie En Rose, realized it was the room and not the performer and asked Dorothy to go to New York and into their club.

At the time La Vie En Rose was in financial trouble. They presented the situation to her up front and honestly. The club was in trouble. It might fold. Dorothy would have to take little money, but if she did well, she'd get a bonus. Dorothy was anxious to get out of Miami where colored people were held in such low esteem. She wanted to be free again, to live and eat where she wanted to.

Too, she had never appeared alone in New York. She wanted that challenge. It was a definite move up the stairway to the stars, or, at least a move upward from where she was. And all because of an unfinished club and segregation.

You can believe in fate or not, yet in Dorothy's case it appeared that usually when she was troubled, circumstances became such that she was rewarded in some way. At least she wanted to believe this is how it happens.

She was a Negro and proud of it. But she never could sing jazz or rhythm and blues. Her music never fitted into the neighborhood ghetto club. The couple of times she thought of it or tried it, it didn't work.

Dorothy did her best in the white world. In actuality, Dorothy was the perfect ambassador for the Negro race. She was a lady, beautiful, thoughtful, eternally good-humored, and she always insisted on the same treatment for herself, her pianist and her maid, sometimes white, sometimes black, as white people were given. She was nearly always successful at it.

The New York La Vie En Rose engagement was a smash hit. It stretched out for fourteen weeks, and her gross was even larger than that of the big stars who were appearing at the Copa, then the most important night spot in New York.

The long run gave her super confidence. Also, it did one more thing. She spent her days doing promotion for her new act and important, sophisticated newsmen were constantly badgering her with questions that had to be answered. They explored the black-white question to the point of stark realism.

Dorothy parried many questions and answered many, too. She was a Negro coping in a white world and she wanted her sister and her mother and her Negro friends to be proud of her and she meant it. She came to believe that everything she did, good or bad, would reflect on her race. She was carefully elegant. She didn't drink, smoke or date publicly, and she never sought the spotlight. She exercised religiously and was never seen socially with a boss because she thought it might be construed that she was having an affair with him.

Dorothy made it a point to always look conservatively formal and well-groomed when she was out. She was always immaculate. She learned quickly how to handle newsmen and important people.

Dorothy told me: "I read once in Time Magazine that when Harry Cohn, chief of Columbia Studios, signed Kim Novak, he told her, 'Remember it won't do you any good to sleep with any of those S.O.B.'s on the lot. The only one it will help to sleep with is me.'"

For some remote reason this story danced through her mind when Ron Toppel, manager of the sprawling but plush El Rancho Hotel in Las Vegas, told her it was Harry Cohn who had asked him to star her in the five-hundred-seat main dining room. I had wondered who waved the magic wand that whisked her from three figures at the broken down Bingo, to a fat four figures at the El Rancho. Dorothy's own words tell it best:

"So now I knew," Dorothy told me. "I was grateful but leery. Ron said casually after the big show opening, 'Harry Cohn's upstairs in his office. He'd like to talk to you personally now.'

"I was only twenty-three, but I was learning about the art of defense, conversational or physical. That was an area in which I had a lot of confidence. You can't be pretty and colored without innocently inviting half of all the men you come in contact with to lust.

"From my early teens I had wanted a romance to be just a simple idealistic thing, but instead it was always a game of fox and hounds, with me as the fox, of course.

"Ron showed me to a private elevator which surprisingly whisked me right into Mr. Cohn's office. There was the great man sitting behind his desk in pajamas and dressing gown.

"He didn't mention or excuse his strange costume, nor did I.

"'Ah, Miss Dandridge,' he said politely, half rising and holding his hand out for a flick of a handshake. He then gestured to a green-flowered stuffed chair.

"I sat down with a thank you and he smiled. 'So this is the lovely Dorothy Dandridge in the flesh. I saw you on the screen and I told the boys, fine bones, delicacy, lovely soft flesh. Too bad it's an illusion. In person, as with all entertainers, somewhere, the dollar sign will show. I was wrong. And, young lady, I am not often wrong. You are beautiful.'

"I could accept his little speech in either of two ways—take the pretty words at face value and politely thank him, or follow my instincts and call it for what it was—a few compliments to soften me up for the kill. And I recognized the man, the pajamas, the tune and the setting for what it was, background for seduction. I never liked to be thought of as dumb, because I wasn't.

In matters of sex I felt I was every bit as clever as he was. If there were any propositions to be made, let them be declared frankly and honestly.

"'Mr. Cohn,' I said, 'you are a very important man. Head of a major studio. Maker of stars. Feared by enemies. I've heard many of the stories. I respect you. So to show my respect, I would like to say what I have to say without any shilly-shally. You were influential in getting me a very important job and I'm very grateful.'

"He held up his hand in a gesture as if to say, 'It was nothing.'

"I went on. 'But you haven't bought me for what you did for me. I'm sensitive about being a colored girl—maybe too sensitive. So be it. Because I'm an attractive Negro does not give you or anyone the license to take me to bed five minutes after you shake my hand for the first time.' I felt perfectly at ease. I wasn't angry. I recognized a worthy adversary in this eternal game of cat and mouse and he was going to find this dark mouse something more than a pushover.

"His reaction was a strange one. He picked up the phone, dialed two numbers and said, 'Burt, get me some chicken legs, cole slaw and cream soda, two bottles. My guest will have ...' He looked at me.

"I was hungry so why not. 'Corned beef sandwich on rye, not fat, mustard, pickles and peppers.'

"He repeated my order. Then he got up and paced.

"'You kids,' he said almost disgustedly. 'I have forty beautiful girls under contract. If I laid all of them once a week I'd have no time to make pictures. Why is it that there are so few girls left you can say a compliment to without them taking off their clothes or resenting you or hating you for it.'

"For the first time I noticed there was a riding crop on his desk. He picked it up and slapped the desk with it noisily, even angrily.

"I didn't believe this behavior. It was reverse psychology. He was using a different strategy, as a chess master would to check my opening move. Yet he had planted the slightest doubt in my mind.

"He paced. 'I saw you in a lousy picture. *Tarzan's Peril*, or something like that. If I made a picture like that, I'd take out full-page ads in the trade papers to apologize to the public. Yet in all that mixture of monkeys and manure, I saw one thing sparkle— you. I don't say I saw any Sarah Bernhardt, but I saw something—a look, a gesture, a tone, something that stopped my ass from hurting. You were on the screen and suddenly I stopped squirming.' He hit the desk again to punctuate his opinion.

"He continued, 'I have a responsibility to my exhibitors, my public and my stockholders. When I see an entertainer who I think has a future, it is my duty to see that Columbia Pictures further explores that entertainer. Whatever you believe, that's why I got you the job here and that's why you are in this room now.'

"He was aware there was one element in our confrontation that, as far as I was concerned, was a false note in his apparent sincerity. He went about correcting it. 'The pajamas and dressing gown in an office? I was up at six this morning to see rushes. I fought with a major star over a contract. I worked out a promotion campaign for a picture of ours that is a stinker. I got a member of my family not to fight a speeding charge and pay the two dollars.' He smiled. 'All day long I've been solving old problems and helplessly watching new ones form. I've been eating aspirins like halva. Then I flew up here, dictated thirty letters from the steam bath, told Burt I was going to bed and to wake me up after the show. I didn't want to see the show in my dead-assed condition. I didn't feel I had to put on white tie and tails for you.' He smiled again.

"The elevator opened and Burt, a handsome young man, brought in our food. He worked quietly placing it on a table for us. It smelled appetizing. He never said a word and walked out quietly when he was finished.

Mr. Cohn seemed to think Burt required some explanation. 'He was an actor. I had him under contract. But nothing happened. You'd be surprised the way the public is sensitive to what it wants. I have to be a thermometer. Something inside of me has to register heat or cold for every picture or actor the public sees. Burt turned out to be a cold salmon. But I like him—personally, I mean. So he works for me.' He took a big bite of chicken, stuffed some cole slaw in with it and suggested, 'Eat. After a day of formalities I always suggest that come midnight, we relax.'

"I did eat and it was good. I was a little impressed by this opinionated, talkative, ego-ridden, so-called tyrant of Gower Street. I realized there was a simpatico between us. In a half hour we were friends and I didn't like it. It was too fast. I didn't trust him or, for that matter, any man. I resented the situation.

"'Mr. Cohn,' I said, 'I must admit that you puzzle me in one way. You have not tried to ply me with drinks like everyone else does.' I guess I said it bitterly and sarcastically because his reaction was anger. 'You know, we colored girls just naturally are supposed to drop our panties when we get some alcohol in us.'

"'I feel a little sorry for you. How do you exist without believing somebody—your mother, your sister, anybody—the television announcer with his commercials.' He burped without excusing himself. 'That's what will eventually destroy the colored race. Not the treatment they get, but the treatment they expect to get.'

"The phone rang. It was three o'clock in the morning. He put his hand over the receiver and said, 'From Paris. It's lunch time there tomorrow.' He became involved in a long conversation about a French actor named Jean-Paul Belmondo, and used an occasional French word in his long speeches about salaries. He said over his hand to me, 'They don't understand much

English.' He seemed pleased after he put the phone down.

"'I shouldn't tell you this, but I will. The management was very happy over your performance tonight.' Then he laughed, spluttering some food about. 'If there are any bonuses to be distributed, they might give one to me for discovering you.'

"The phone rang again and he told the switchboard operator not to put through any more calls until six a.m. I wondered how he could get along on less than three hours sleep. The few times I had done it, my voice became a rasping whisper the next day.

"We finished our food and the man who headed a multi-million dollar empire paced in his purple dressing gown.

"'You don't need me,' he offered. 'You have enough of what it takes to make it on your own. I've made a lot of big stars—Rita Hayworth, Glen Ford, Kim Novak—just to name a few. I know how to do it. There's one boss. Me. I don't want my actors to think. I just want them to follow orders. That's what I would do with you. Make a star out of you. Oh yes, there are some whining exhibitors down South who complain when we use a Negro in a picture, but we ram it down their throats. There are ways. And if they don't like it, we yank the Columbia franchise.' He punctuated the threat with one big fist hitting his open hand.

"He was so sincere about it I felt like thanking him for a crisis that might not ever come to pass.

"'I have a confession to make,' he said, his voice becoming softer. 'When I first saw you on the screen, I had a hard-on for you. Who the hell wouldn't! All that quiet sex wrapped up in a cute brown bundle. You reached the old man, I'll tell you. But the moment I saw you in the flesh, I was aware that you had something more. You were a person of three dimensions.' Suddenly he smiled and stopped pacing. 'All right,' he said, 'that will be enough for tonight. It's getting late.'

"He was dismissing me! And no pass! I was flabbergasted. I got up and suddenly I was confused. Would this be the last time I would see and talk to this giant of the entertainment industry – a man who, by just saying so, would make me a star? I was panicked.

"He took me quietly by the arm and we walked to the elevator. For the first time all evening he had nothing to say.

"And for the first time in years with a man, I was at a loss as to how to save what could be an important relationship. With every step I was accenting a lost chance.

"We reached the elevator and neither of us moved. He still smiled. 'You have to push the button,' he said. 'Not yet have they perfected an automatic light beam for elevators.' I knew what he meant. When I pushed that button, it signified my career at Columbia Pictures was through before it began. Seconds were ticking.

"He looked at me and he pushed it. Finished! He still smiled. The elevator arrived and the door opened. I just stood there but there was no movement. He took me by the arm and led me back to the chair, and gently tapped me so I sat down.

"He stood over me and talked. 'You want success? How much do you want success? One hundred percent? Seventy-five percent? Fifty percent? Let me tell you something, young lady, with your pride, the dignity, the love of race, the morality, you have chosen some expensive qualities. Success makes no bargain. You give her one hundred percent or no dice. Sure, it would be nice to become a big star on your own terms, but it doesn't happen that way.

"'When you didn't push that elevator button, it was just as if you said loud and clear, Harry, I want you to go to bed with me. I want to make you happy so you will make a famous actress out of me. I heard you—every word.'

"I started to deny it but he held up his hand. 'You

made a big point of our having an honest relationship. Don't spoil it. Not pressing that elevator button was just like taking off your clothes. Now *I'm* going to be honest. As you suggested, I invited you here for one reason, to lay you. Every word I have spoken here, every action I have made was designed for that purpose. Even though at times you had some doubts, you were always right.'

"He began pacing again. 'Young lady, I am a very shrewd man. I am at my best with people. More than with things. It is my business to look at a beautiful girl like you and in a few minutes know exactly what my goal is and what strategy I will use to attain it. And I don't fail, ever!'

"There was no fight left. I could only sit and wait for his verdict. In a way, he had stripped off all feminine subterfuge. He had forced me to be honest with myself.

"'It's like this,' he went on. 'I think you will become a very successful entertainer and actress. We'll be friends for a long time. I want you to go to bed with me but I can't make you any promises. I may never have the opportunity to put you into a picture. That's the way it is. But then again, if you'll gamble, I might be of great help to you.

"'The way I see it, you have to gamble. In fact, in every situation like this—*if it is genuine*—you must gamble.'

"He stood over me. 'I'm going to sleep now, alone, in bungalow double A. I am very tired and cole slaw always gives me heartburn. But if you'd like to pay me a visit there tomorrow evening after your first show, I would be delighted to play host.'

"In one hour or so, I realized I had become fond of him. I kissed him on the cheek, told him I'd be happy to be his guest, and left."

"What did you do the next evening," I asked.

"The next evening I did go to his bungalow. I

found Harry Cohn, with all his vulgarities and earthiness, to be a fascinating human being. I never worked at Columbia Pictures again, but when you gamble, you lose as often as you win. That's the nature of the game."

I asked Dottie about her family background. She said her mother was born in the USA but she was part Jamaican, Indian and Mexican, and that her father was half African and half white. We figured out she was part African, Jamaican, Spanish, Indian and Caucasian. I said, "That's probably the world of the future, a mixture of all races. It seems to work in Latin America, Hawaii and other places." The black is beautiful concept came much later.

Dottie said, "In the United States you are prejudiced against if you are anything other than White, Anglo-Saxon, and Protestant. Herb Jeffries is just as black as Ma Rainey. We're all really black."

Then she met her match. She played Rio and after a few days among strangers became restless. She loved this warm and colorful country. Although she was lonely, she was comfortable because most of the people were her color and many wealthy Brazilians were darker than she. She later learned there is class prejudice in Brazil and that the blacks were in extreme poverty and treated cruelly.

She met Christian Marcos at a swank cocktail party. He had been pointed out to her as a famous industrialist who owned a large hunk of Brazil. He was terribly complimentary to her and his charm overwhelmed her.

She had only one show a night at the Rio Copa which left her a lot of time. His chauffeured car took her for long drives through the tropics and she saw Rio through his eyes. His beautiful beach home, his city home, his mountain home all overpowered her. She had never seen anything like this.

And the more time she spent with him, the more

important she found he was. Her letters home were full of romantic fervor:

"Dear Earl:

"Christian and I seem alone in this tropical paradise and I dread the inevitable parting. Or is it inevitable? Why couldn't I give up my career, marry and live in South America or Mexico—he owns much property there, too.

"Oh, I'm so torn yet so happy. Am I really Negro, Earl? He never mentions it. Takes me everywhere, introduces me to everyone, and proudly. It's a beautiful dream and I hope I never awake.

"When each day is through and I go to bed I think of what a wonderful day it was and how nothing can ever be as marvelous again. Yet the next day is even better. Sometimes I think I'm not entitled to all this happiness. Yet Christian says I am a symbol of love and symbols are always the same, for him anyway...."

Being a practical man by virtue of the profession I was in, I prayed nothing would topple her castle of happiness, but I feared the worst. Not that I felt any impending doom but only because such happiness always must end.

How right I was, yet I was surprised when it happened.

When she returned she explained their last night together. He had been called on business to Mexico City.

"My run was ending at the Copa. My next stop was Sao Paulo. Christian called me several times and begged me to take an early morning flight and stay with him just for a day. It was hectic but I flew to Mexico City and he met me at the airport.

"He had reserved a suite for me at the Reforma. He told me we would dine at his home. His home was magnificent, the rooms larger than many of the clubs where I had worked. I looked at him there in his plush natural habitat and thought how he exuded happiness and success. His zest for life was always refreshing.

"He took me through his home, proud of the fine art and the antiques. The view from the terrace was inspiring. I suppose I must have misinterpreted his enthusiasm because I translated it all to mean that this would be the home we'd live in as man and wife.

"As we looked out over the valley bay he said gently, 'Couldn't you be happy this way all your life?'

"I answered truthfully that I wanted nothing else. This was enough. He squeezed me gently and said, 'You shall have it.'

"This was the peak feeling of my life. How I loved him!

"What followed after that was a nightmare made more so by the contrast to what had gone before.

"I suppose the lines of communication had been poor between us. Perhaps because when you want to believe a certain thing, you shut out everything else. He said dreamily, 'My wife and children are in Europe, that's why it seems so peaceful here. Obviously we cannot have this house. But I will buy a house just as big and luxurious for you. Wherever you want it. I am sure you will be happy on, say, $200,000 a year. I want to give you so large an allowance because I'd like you to give up your career.'

"Because of my silence he sensed something was not quite right, but he was wrong as to what was bothering me.

"He said, 'I will be with you more than with my family. However, you will be free to travel and spend what you wish. When you want me, you need only call me.'

"I knew I shouldn't cry. My pride was at stake. The only way I could keep from crying was to remain silent. He held me close believing I had been convinced this would be my way of life. Several times I tried to talk and couldn't.

"When he went out on a short business appoint-

ment, I left. There was a note, yes. I left a very simple
note for him. 'I love you. I wanted to be your wife.
Anything less than that wouldn't work.'

"I'll never see him again."

Dorothy finished her engagement at the Copa. She
just went through the motions. Then she went like a
wounded bird to Sao Paulo where she just played out
the engagement.

Back home we got her to a good psychiatrist
because she was highly distraught. South American
doctors had prescribed sedatives and she was eating
them like candy.

Dorothy was a sensitive soul and the romantic incident in South America had felled her like a stricken
bird. She needed help so badly it was questionable if
she could work if she didn't get it.

What psychiatry did for her was create a strange
quirk that made her constantly talk of "the right man"
and "the right marriage." But this hope brought her
back to a semblance of normalcy again. She believed all
her insecurities and moods were due to her not having
the right marriage—when she achieved that, she'd be
happy forevermore.

I am often asked if psychiatry helped Dottie and
why she needed it. I dug up a letter from her psychiatrist that she received while she was appearing at the
Statler Hotel in Boston in March of 1954:

March 16, 1954

My dear Dorothy:

It was very pleasant talking to you over the telephone. You are working through a very difficult period
in your analysis. When you were a little girl you were
hurt when your father and your aunt turned away from
you. They did not give you the love, affection and the
attention you needed. You were hurt very much and
severely so. As a defense against this pain your sub-
conscious mind told you, "If I had not cared for them in
the first place I would not have been hurt. The pain I

suffer is due to my love for them....But I cannot depend upon them to love me. I loved them once but they were unfaithful to me. If I do not love them then I cannot be hurt."

The above process conditioned you to stay aloof from people and not to form close personal relationships. The few times that you have tried you have been "burned" again.These rejections of your present life touch subconsciously upon the original pain.

As a child you were small, your little mind could not stand all your true feelings about how badly you were hurt so most of the feelings about what these people did to you remained unconscious.

Today, when you meet someone you like you put up the same fight as you did as a child. You say "If I do not like him he cannot hurt me. If I run away or even hurt him I will pay him back for what the others did to me and what he may do to me."

At present if you allow yourself to fall into this trap you are repeating your infantile pattern. You will never break the pattern.As an adult you must learn to tolerate a certain amount of rejection. You must reflect upon your childhood years. Can you remember your parents rejecting you? Can you recapture the feelings and the emotions from your childhood rejections? Who else rejected you? Did others turn away from you? Even being born is interpreted by the infant's unconscious as a rejection. "I was pushed out into the cold hostile world. Now I must ward off these hurts myself instead of mother protecting me. I must breathe for myself and feed myself whereas mother used to do these things for me through the umbilical cord." The cutting of the cord is interpreted as castration, a separation from the mother which the child thinks of as part of itself.

When the mother toilet trains the child the child interprets it as rejection. "If mother loved me she would not make me do these things. She would let me do the things that are instinctive in me. She would say a kind word instead of scolding me."

Sometimes a person unconsciously allows herself to fall into a situation so that she manages to get hurt. By doing so she repeats the original hurt. Then it is like being a baby again. "I am being hurt as I was hurt when I was a child. If I am hurt I am a child. If I am a child, I will have the advantages of being a child. No responsibilities, protection, and it will allow me to seek the pleasures I still have within me which were never gratified."

If you write out your associations, do not censor them. If you have time put them in an envelope and mail them to me. I will analyze them and mail the reply to you.

Have a nice opening in Boston and have some fun. When you return to L.A. I look forward with pleasure to seeing you.
Kind personal regards,
Jack

Dorothy Dandridge as a teacher in *Bright Road*, a low budget production by
Dore Schary, then head of production at MGM. Actually the studio was hoping
the offbeat movie would break even which it did not do at first.Later it made
big bucks when Dorothy and co-star Harry Belafonte became famous.

CHAPTER
NINE

Dorothy was destined not to have a happy marriage. It was strange. In personal endeavors, such as her career and associations with people, she had a drive that demanded success and she achieved it. Whatever she wanted, really wanted, she seemed to get. But when it came to marriage, it was nothing but failure.

We could even go outside the bounds of marriage. Her romances—and there weren't many of them—ended the same way, in dismal failure. She would talk about it. She always thought there was something a little wrong with what she did or said that caused problems but in actuality she chose the wrong men, a common fault among many beautiful women.

She was a great admirer of physical masculinity, of masculine strength. Actually she put too much accent on that particular characteristic of a man. Each time she had an unhappy relationship with a man the moodiness spilled over onto her work, which was affected badly. Had she been able to control her romantic situations she would have been a much happier star, but then the qualities that made Dorothy Dandridge complex brought both success and failure.

In June of 1952 Dorothy Dandridge went back to

Cleveland, where she had lived a good part of her early life, to make a series of appearances for the Alhambra Club—a Negro organization.

Perhaps it was her childhood that demanded she try to help her race or just natural compassion for people, but it was constantly on her mind. Many times she went to great expense of energy and time to do things for Negroes.

While she was in Cleveland, she was signed for a major starring role in MGM's *See How They Run*. It was a project being pushed by then studio head, Dore Schary. Dore was a very social minded man interested in the interracial question and wanted to do a movie about black human beings without attaching any harsh propaganda to it. He felt Dorothy, with her beauty and her soft facade, was perfect to play a compassionate Negro school teacher.

The picture was taken from a Christopher Award-winning short story by the black writer, Mary Margaret Vroman. The news of the signing of Dorothy for the picture, one of the first to be made by a major studio and starring Negroes in a non-musical, excited the whole Negro community. They were impressed and happy that the blacks had suddenly got Hollywood to do something with dignity for them. The actors would not be entertainers or maids, waiters and bus boys.

For Dorothy it was a great triumph that she was selected for the role, for many reasons. She always felt that she could present herself best on screen and, secondly, it was a wonderful opportunity for her to star in an MGM non-singing film. It could also calm the critics in the black community who felt she had aligned herself exclusively with the white community because she almost always appeared exclusively in clubs catering to whites.

At the peak of all this excitement and publicity, one day in Cleveland she was stopped by a distinguished looking Negro man with a very pleasant smile.

He approached her almost shyly and said, without any introduction, "Hello, Dorothy. I am your father."

This was Cyril Dandridge who had left home and divorced her mother, Ruby, before she was born. She had never seen him. Actually she had carried some resentment toward him because she had no father to make her childhood more normal. She hated the aunt who disciplined and beat her constantly all of her youthful years.

She was surprised and delighted to see him. It was one of the mysteries of life, finally solved. She hugged him and they chatted for a while. Cyril Dandridge was doing well and married. He wanted nothing from Dorothy. Only to be proud of her. She realized quickly that he was someone she could come to if she needed him. Actually, other than that warm meeting of several minutes, they never talked again in person. He did have a chance to tell her how proud he was of her. She was overwhelmed with feeling. Dorothy was an emotional, sentimental girl anyway and to be standing there with her father, seeing him for the first time, filled her with every sort of feeling.

For a couple of days she could talk only of her father and that meeting. She was thirty when they first met although she had thought of him many times over the years. She told everyone how nice her father was. It was the first opportunity she had ever had to say something like that.

The title of *See How They Run* was changed to *Bright Road*. Dorothy approached the role with a great deal of enthusiasm. She was convinced she was primarily an actress and secondarily a singer. Her co-star was Harry Belafonte and a long and good friendship developed between them. He was married at the time or something more might have come of their friendship. They truly loved each other, each telling anyone who would listen how wonderful the other one was. They got along fine during the picture and, in fact, made another one together.

The picture, *Bright Road*, was a great experience for Dorothy. It renewed her confidence in her relationship with men. She liked her director, Gerald Mayer. He was very understanding of her not only as a sensitive actress, but as a troubled mother of a retarded child, and a sincere artist who strived for perfection. She felt comfortable with him. She felt easier about her friendships with white men. They had great respect for each other.

It's strange, but once again an incident which appeared to be a killer and detrimental to her career happened about this time and actually helped her a great deal in her career.

Fate has a strange way of working out lives and often puts the pieces of the puzzle together before the conclusion of an event. If that sounds complicated, note what Dorothy's best friend, actor Joel Fluellon, and another friend, a prominent Negro attorney named Leo Branton, accomplished for her.

About this time a scandal magazine broke a big story about a young white musician who told the magazine that once he'd asked Dorothy to take a walk with him through the woods in Lake Tahoe and she submitted happily to his advances on the greens.

Because Dorothy was so sensitive about black-white relations, and she was a lady and the story was a lie, she felt she had to do something about either suing the magazine or getting them to run some kind of denial. Others in the picture industry advised her not to make a fuss over it. "It is good publicity," they said. Many more stars had been demeaned by the magazine and had decided that aired in court, it could only hurt them. They felt that everyone has something in their lives to hide and while they might disprove one thing, other things might be brought out.

But Dorothy felt she had nothing to hide and she

was willing to put her life on the line, as it were. So she sued the magazine. After much publicity and legal maneuvering, the magazine made an apology and a payment of $10,000 to her for the embarrassment they had caused. It was also made clear that the story was untrue.

Dorothy had her moment of triumph. The incident catapulted her into the public eye again and her image remained intact, that of a heartbreakingly beautiful Negro, intent upon showing the white world that a woman of color could be talented, successful, and something other than a quick lay.

Bright Road had a small budget but nevertheless great care was taken with the making of the picture. It was a favored Dore Schary must and everyone connected with it tried to do him and it justice.

Bright Road contained many dramatic scenes. One, in particular, was a death scene of a child. It gave Dorothy a chance to show many emotions and many times she'd break down in a scene and cry real tears when she was supposed to.

Her heart was in the interest of blacks, especially as translated to children, so that she could honestly feel the role. Also, during the making of the picture she confided that many times the children made her aware of Harolyn, her own retarded daughter, and it would set her to sobbing.

Just before Dorothy was about to begin work in *Bright Road,* we were called to meet with a representative of Nicholas M. Schenck, president of Loews, Inc., and she was handed a list of questions to answer. She was one of the many artists suspected of being involved in what the House Committee On UnAmerican Activities believed to be reasons for her to be blacklisted which would cause her to be unable to work in films.

I must say some employees at MGM were critical of the questions and offered suggestions regarding answering them. Although these were not officials, their suggestions were helpful. No one would tell me who wanted these answers nor who prepared the questions. We couldn't face her accusers nor the accuracy of the allegations. The prospect of Dorothy being blacklisted was strange. She was a very beautiful and talented girl who loved people and one who was friendly to anyone that was decent and friendly towards her. She was never involved in politics.

I discussed the questions at length with Dorothy and her close friends, such as Harold and Mildred Jovien, who were always helpful to her in any way they could be.

The exact questions and Dorothy's answers, in part influenced by what we were told to say, follows:

July 11, 1952
Mr. Nicholas M. Schenck, President
Loew's, Inc.
1540 Broadway
New York, N.Y.

Dear Mr. Schenck:
Certain newspaper reports have been brought to my attention which I would like to comment on.

1. PW 3/14/47 – *One Dorothy Dandridge will appear at a party Saturday night, March 22nd at 2118 Hobart Street, Los Angeles, auspices National Negro Congress.*

I appeared at this party believing that the National Negro Congress was associated with the National Association for the Advancement of Colored People (NAACP), a well recognized organization. I went with my husband, Harold Nicholas. I went for social reasons and because I was interested in the Negro community. I honestly can't remember who asked us to attend.

2. PW 6/30/47 – *Dorothy Dandridge among those who*

spoke at a series of rallies sponsored by the Progressive Citizens of America protesting the Taft-Hartley bill.

I did not speak, however, I might have been considered a member since I was requested to make a donation and I donated a small amount. I was asked to sing by a member of the program committee, whose name I can't remember. As an entertainer, I have been asked by hundreds of organizations during the past seven years to appear at benefits, the names of the individuals requesting my appearance have long since been forgotten with this event as well as numerous others such as the Catholic Youth Organization, B'nai B'rith Brotherhood Week, Red Cross, Cerebral Palsy, Heart Campaign, Pittsburgh Courier, women's clubs that I appeared for. I only remember this as one of over a hundred benefit appearances I have made and just another benefit. All five of these newspaper articles greatly magnify my appearance with these organizations and it is my feeling that they used my name for their own particular advantage and without any authorization.

3. PW 9/17/47 – *One Dorothy Dandridge, actress, on ballot for executive board of Hollywood Arts, Sciences and Professions Council.*

I was a member of the Hollywood Arts, Sciences and Professions Council. I voluntarily became a member when I read that several prominent personalities in show business were active, such as Al Jarvis and Norman Corwin. I believed it would further my career and that it would help members of my race. I never held nor sought an office with this organization nor was I an active member.

4. PW 9/10/48 – *One Dorothy Dandridge student of Actor's Lab.*

Yes, I joined the Actor's Lab because this workshop was one of the few outlets available to a young actress of my race seeking actual workshop training. Attending the Lab was in direct relationship with my theatrical ambition.

5. DW 9/4/51 – *One Dorothy Dandridge, young Negro actress, student at the Lab has commented "As an actress and student at the Lab, I am anxious to know whether Hedda Hopper considers the democratic policy of the Lab, wherein students are accepted on ability, a subversive policy. If she does she advocates a policy which is un-American and fans the flames of race hatred.*

I noticed the date of this alleged quotation in 1951. First of all, I was not a student at the Lab at this time and to my knowledge the Lab was no longer in existence at this date. I recall one incident regarding Hedda Hopper while I was a student at the Lab. What Hedda Hopper said did affect me and I did express concern. However, the exact wording of this particular quotation is not the kind of language I use but I'm sure no one could object to my expressing concern.

I would like to close by saying that I am not now or ever have been a member of the Communist Party or Communist Party Political Association nor have I ever made any donations to these parties. Had I known that any of the above organizations would later be cited as Communistic and or subversive I would never have participated. I have at no time been active politically. My sole interests are towards having a successful career and aiding my people.

Sincerely,

/s/ dorothy dandridge

Dorothy Dandridge

P.S. I would be most agreeable to meet and discuss the above with anybody that you may designate.

Although she was totally apolitical, Dorothy had to account for many of her activities in Hollywood as she was one of the many artists suspected of being involved in what the House Committee On UnAmerican Activities believed to be "Communist Fronts."

Bright Road was on a short shooting schedule of actually about seventeen days. MGM knew there would be problems selling the picture. The South was still adamant about showing Negroes as human beings. In fact, they were adamant about a picture even dealing with a Negro. But MGM felt that the picture, if it broke even, could do a great deal for the public relations of the studio.

Studios, through the years, had felt that an all-Negro film, especially not a musical or an Uncle Tom film, would be banned from all the white theaters in the South. But actually there was something about *Bright Road*, which title was now on the picture, that made the fear unjustified. It was a little picture. Not one to cause any sensation or to make waves, and theater exhibitors gave it a chance.

Reviews were excellent and Dore Schary was delighted. He threw a large party and Dorothy was surrounded by press and photographers. The picture was a modest success financially and everyone was very happy about it. It immediately set everyone looking for another movie for Dorothy.

Reviews such as *"Bright Road* is a unique, offbeat picture that has its touching moments and overall charm. Dorothy Dandridge is beautiful and a good actress," certainly didn't hurt the film.

We might point out here that in its first run the picture didn't do the business they expected it to do, but as soon as Dorothy Dandridge and Harry Belafonte became more popular, more money came into the coffers.

MGM won the George Washington Carver Award for the picture.

Dorothy's first statement to the press was, "This is the first movie to show Negroes as just people. I think it will do more than the 'problem' picture. A white girl could sit in the audience and think, 'This school teacher could be me.'"

Dorothy was pleased because the picture showed Negroes in roles other than servants. She said, "Certainly there are colored maids. There are white maids, too. But there should be a counter-balance. There are also Negro teachers and doctors and architects. Negroes should have those roles, too. They would just be there—as a clerk in a department store, a secretary, a typist. I could play a clerk who gets involved in a murder mystery for example. After all, in real life I come in contact with white persons every day."

During the picture, producer Sol Fielding said, "The picture is being made economically. The Negro audience will pay for the picture." Dorothy beamed. If the Negro audience could pay for a picture, the studios could make many pictures with Negroes in it. If one of these pictures could just get a slice of the white audience, it would make money.

Dorothy was happy during the making of this picture, even though though the producer didn't think Dorothy was dark enough to play a Negro. She had to go to makeup to become a darker shade of brown.

This was Dorothy's third straight dramatic film. Belafonte did two songs in the picture.

Once, Louis B. Mayer, MGM chieftain, came on the set. He pleased Dorothy by saying, "So this is the sexy, sultry, satiny night club singer." Dorothy was dressed in typical conservative school teacher clothes and looked nothing like a sexy singer.

She could hold her own with Mayer: "And so you're the benevolent chief of Metro. I'm an actress that can do any kind of role."

They shook hands.

"All I ask from you," he said, "is a good performance. I don't care anything about sex appeal. I don't ask for anything more than devotion to duty."

But he patted her on the fanny when he left.

The first time Mayer saw the rushes he called Dorothy into his office. She reported the confrontation to me.

"Sit down," Mayer said.

She sat.

He chewed on a toothpick. "It's like this," he said. "Some girls have it and some don't. You do. But here's what I want you to do. I want you to look prim and proper just like you've been doing. But I want you to think sexy. You'd be surprised how even a prim and proper girl can look if she thinks sexy. You know what I mean?"

Dorothy said she did.

"You practice it," he said. "I don't have to tell you girls. You all know how to do that. You're born with it."

Dorothy said she would practice it thought she did know how to think sexy.

Mayer seemed to want to talk. He shut off the phone calls. "The industry is ready for a Negro actress. A sexy one but with class. Lena Horne had it but she wasn't interested in becoming an actress. It's my opinion that the white fears the black. If there is any tension or aggression in a Negro actor's face, that's the end. You have the perfect qualities for success – placidity, beauty, refinement and sex. And they're blended well."

"Thank you," Dorothy said.

Mayer paced. "In my opinion, you can become the highest paid Negro actor or actress in movie history. I know it. I feel it in my rump where I always feel the future."

Louis B. Mayer was almost right. Sidney Poitier became one of the highest paid stars in Hollywood although Dorothy earned $125,000 and $100,000 per film before Poitier did.

Dorothy was very excited. She could see herself as the biggest star in the firmament. It was breathtaking.

Mayer went on talking: "We're going to promote you, Dorothy. And when a giant studio like MGM gets behind you, it's almost sure you'll be big—very big.

Then we're going to promote the picture. You watch. You'll be surprised and pleased with our efforts."

Trouble was Mayer was starting to lose his hold on the studio and while his intentions were good, the promotion he spoke of never happened. Not only was Dorothy neglected but so was the picture.

But Dorothy glowed. With such promising words coming from the man who ran the studio, she'd have nothing to worry about anymore. Dorothy, like most Hollywood actresses, never allowed for a change in the scheme of things. When things were good, she expected them to be good forever. When things were bad, the same. And she acted accordingly.

She was with Mayer about an hour while he talked on: "I'll tell you the trick of success. Whatever you gain you hold onto grimly like a mountain climber. If you slip back you can fall and that's the end of you. You must hold tight to each gain and concentrate on your success.

"Take you, for instance. *Bright Road* could make you one of Hollywood's biggest stars. If it does, get yourself a good press agent, manager, business manager, secretary. But put the pressure on. Spend money wisely. And when scripts are submitted, do what the studio tells you to do. They know best. Actresses get big heads and think they know everything. That's the beginning of the end. Being a Negro you'll have to be doubly careful. Don't say 'no' to your studio. They'll do what's best for you. Don't be arrogant. But then I don't have to tell you that. You're a sweet girl. Do I?"

Dorothy sweetly told him she'd cooperate all the way. She meant it, too.

Mayer glowed, "You know about my big happy family at MGM. Well, we welcome you to our arms. This is the first time we've had a pretty Negro actress with us. We're delighted to have you become a part of the family.

MGM signed Dorothy for a musical guest spot in *It*

Remains To Be Seen. It was a small part but it showed their faith in her, and it helped her career.

Reviews for Bright Road were excellent and Dore Schary of MGM was delighted. He threw a large party and Dorothy was surrounded by press and photographers. The picture was a modest success financially. It immediately set everyone looking for another movie for Dorothy. MGM won the George Washington Carver Award (Mr. Carver, a distinguished educator, is pictured opposite. (Dorothy is shown in another scene from the film on page 121.) Dorothy's statement to the press was, "This is the first movie to show Negroes as just ordinary people."

In rehearsal for her show at the Riviera in Las Vegas where she would meet her second husband, Jack Dennison. By this time she was a top draw and making over $10,000 a week in clubs a huge salary for the times. She felt it was time for her to take a crack at the movies.

CHAPTER
TEN

Dorothy went to the same drama school, the Actor's Lab, as Marilyn Monroe did. At the time the odds would have been millions to one that either would ever star in a movie, let alone do what they both did.

Marilyn, at the time, wanted to do musical shows. Dorothy was only interested in heavy drama. Later on, Marilyn changed her mind and wanted to do classics. Dorothy always preferred the dramatic even though she made her reputation as a singer.

Dorothy would often talk of Marilyn and all her life she was influenced by her. Not so much as an actress but as a woman, a human being. Both needed applause more than they needed money. Both were willing to sacrifice anything for career. And both had tragic marriages.

Dorothy would say later on in life, "I never thought of Marilyn as a tragic figure. She was full of joy and excitement for living. Sure, she had her moods, but mostly she was a happy girl. Her problem was in believing. She believed people even after they disappointed her over and over.

"I think her one fault was that she needed people to like her. Not exactly the people she knew and liked, but all people, everybody. Once we went to a party before she became so famous. She was so pretty and gay that everyone showed her a lot of attention.That is, all except a small seven-year-old boy who belonged to the host.

"For some reason, he wouldn't come to Marilyn when she called him. It was important to her that he come to her and like her. She concentrated on him. He was the focal point of the party. She spent hours trying to cultivate him. In the end he got to like her. Then she beamed. The party would have been a dismal flop for her if Marilyn and the small child hadn't become friends."

In a way, Dorothy was like that. To know someone liked her made her happy. To know someone disliked her was tantamount to a minor disaster. She'd brood and even elicit help to try and get back into the good graces of the person who didn't like her.

She admired Marilyn for her great patience, a quality she lacked. In those days, Marilyn was up for a Los Angeles play. Every day Dorothy would ask whether Marilyn got the role. She'd reply gaily, "I don't know yet."

That would bug Dorothy to distraction. She was much more curious, impatient and overwrought than Marilyn and it was Marilyn's part.Then the day came when Dorothy asked the much repeated question, "Did you hear?" and Marilyn replied, "Yes, I got the part."

Dorothy danced for joy. Marilyn merely smiled happily. It was always liked that.

Even when Dorothy was to be chosen for a small part in the school play, she was nervous and upset. Marilyn was full of words like, "You're a sure thing. Just forget it and have fun." Sure enough, Dorothy got the part and Marilyn was quite smug about it.

In matters of romance it was the same thing. Dorothy was impatient to know how everything would turn out. Marilyn was satisfied to drift along and let things take their natural course.

I remember the famous incident when Marilyn Monroe made *Seven Year Itch* and it led to her divorce from Joe DiMaggio. I don't know if you remember it, but Marilyn was doing a scene where she was standing over a subway grating in the sidewalk and the whoosh of the passing subway blew up her skirts.

Joe and Walter Winchell were in New York and walked over at four in the morning to watch the shooting. There was a sparse crowd because of the hour and Joe and Walter were up front to see the scene shot over and over, each time revealing Marilyn's brief panties.

Joe found it humiliating and pulled Walter away after a while. Later that night he was supposed to have lectured Marilyn about dignity in her career.

She sobbed and said he didn't understand her career and he should try to put himself in her place. Joe, of course, couldn't be moved from his stand. They talked through the day and night.

In the end they decided to get a divorce. Obviously, it wasn't the result of the one incident but that was the trigger.

When that happened, Marilyn phoned Dorothy and the two girls cried on the telephone. Dorothy offered help but there was really nothing she could do.

Dorothy even offered to come to New York to help. By that time the marriage was over. Such happenings made Dorothy think. She said, "When I marry again, whatever my husband wants, he can have. I'll dedicate my life to his wishes."

She tried that and she was only taken advantage of. Men, she later philosophized, don't want service. They want variety. Of course, Shakespeare said that long before she did.

Dorothy thought she stood alone among women who could live in heavenly bliss with men she was having an affair with, but have the love disintegrate when she married them. But as I traveled around among the girls of the entertainment business, I heard that cry quite often. I'm sure the complaint is not restricted to the entertainment business.

One night when Dorothy and I were relaxing and she was concerned about Marilyn, we talked about more intimate things. She had this to say: "Marilyn was the sex symbol of the world but I don't think she liked to be that. And furthermore, she didn't think she was so hot in bed. Marilyn always had pains of some kind, so making love for Marilyn was often painful. You can't enjoy sex that way."

It's funny Dorothy said that because she resented being pointed out as a sex symbol. She didn't even think she was sexy. She had to come to the conclusion she was only because many men told her so.

Further on Marilyn, Dorothy said, "What she wanted in a man didn't exist. She had the feeling that the right man could cure all her ills, her insecurities, her doubts. He could protect her from the troubles of the world. Each time she met a man she could fall in love with, she felt this was the man who could do all those things. So she went into a marriage or a relationship filled with great hope.

"Then the man couldn't possibly live up to the things expected of him. Furthermore, he didn't know what was expected of him. If he did, maybe things could have worked out. But actually if asked, Marilyn couldn't have told him what to do to fill her emptiness."

That's what Dorothy said and I thought again how like Dorothy. The very symptoms she understood in Marilyn, she had. Perhaps not as exaggerated but she had the same insecurities.

But to the more intimate. Marilyn liked to be touched by a man. But she didn't like to touch. She was so completely feminine, it was her desire to be made love to but not to make love. It was a problem for a mate because she'd do what he wanted to do but she wouldn't like it.

So he'd never know why she'd never make love to him again. It was a real problem of her sex life. Women are strange. She'd never tell a man her wants or desires. He had to find them out for himself.

Dorothy and I would have talks about why men seemed to be inflamed by her because she was black. They thought black girls were sexier. She didn't know why. Oh, she had guesses. For one, for many white men, the black girl was different, unique. For another reason, the black was forbidden fruit. It was still unusual and provocative to see a black girl with a white man.

Then Dorothy had been told by white men that black girls were better in bed than their white sisters. Reason? Because the black was supposed to be less inhibited. They had no hang-ups about sex, anything went. It was many white men's comment that the average white girl made love for gain, seldom for love. That is for money, gifts, marriage, position and what not. But the black was more honest. She got earthy, basic kicks from sex and she resorted to it for no other reason than gratification.

Dorothy got wound up in discussions like this. Did the black woman understand men better? Were they disappointed, disillusioned or unhappy because men desired them for just one reason--sex? Many of her friends thought that was perfectly honest and resented it not one bit.

Dorothy knew a Negro girl in Watts who practiced prostitution for a living. She was pretty and slim but had nothing to look forward to than a life of prostitution and then perhaps cynicism, narcotics and alcohol.

But she went out on a call one night to a poker game and a middle-aged white stockbroker took a liking to her. He set her up in a nice house and kept her for a while and then, to everyone's surprise, married her. Dorothy loved this story because it proved a point of hers—that a colored girl in Watts could find love anywhere like any other girl.

Dorothy wanted to go back into the clubs and sing again and make big money. Dorothy thrived on work and singing made her work. She went back into the Mocambo and again got great reviews. But now she was restless. She felt she was right on the brink of big stardom and yet she was repeating all the things she had done before. She was ready to take the big step forward but nothing was happening. She started to hate the business end again.

What she didn't know was that it was happening behind her back, not to her knowledge, and it was happening at Twentieth Century Fox Studios. In those days, Darryl Zanuck ruled the studio with an iron hand. He had a history of success and success in Hollywood is law. So whatever he said was done.

Zanuck, at the time, was friendly with independent producer Otto Preminger. Preminger was a man who never lost his accent though he lost his hair. He was always a man full of ideas and doggedly determined about them. He, at one time, was known for his wild and unusual love affairs. One of them was with Dorothy Dandridge, but we'll get to that later on.

Zanuck and Preminger had many meetings. They once had a feud going during which Zanuck swore Preminger would never work again in Hollywood. But all that was patched up. What they were discussing was getting the rights to Oscar Hammerstein's Broadway version of Bizet's *Carmen*. Both would share in the production and in the profits.

It was all decided and then Preminger went back to New York to work with Hammerstein on the screen version of the musical *Carmen*. By the third of March, 1950, he had progressed far enough to announce the forming of his own Carlyle Productions which would co-produce with Twentieth Century Fox. The first announcement of casting was Pearl Bailey who was signed to portray Carmen's girl friend, Frankie, "who lived off the fat heads of the land." She would sing, "Beat Out That Rhythm On The Drums."

The next casting was Harry Belafonte, signed to play the role of Joe, the tragic soldier lured by Carmen to love her and who finally killed her.

Now the big problem for both Zanuck and Preminger was to find a Carmen. Preminger talked to casting people about it. He went through the motion picture academy books and talked to the many stars that had worked with him before. None was quite right.

I met Dorothy at the Los Angeles International Airport that April. She had just closed at the Last Frontier in Las Vegas and had been very successful. Before that she worked at La Vie En Rose in New York at $7,500 a week, which was some kind of record.

She was totally aware that *Carmen* was to be made.

I told her sadly Otto Preminger didn't seem very responsive toward her as Carmen. She was furious. All the way from the airport to home she talked about how she had to have the part. Dorothy was a pretty sweet girl who gave no indication on the surface of what boiled underneath. When she needed and wanted something, every fiber of her being concentrated on it. She was determined to get the role. She felt that it was the best part for a Negro motion picture actress in film history. It was important to her because she felt that if she could get Carmen, it would show the the entire world, and especially the black community how talented she really was. That was always uppermost in her mind.

At the time Dorothy Dandridge's agent was MCA—Music Corporation of America—I was her personal manager. It was up to them to get her motion picture parts so I had gone to them, knowing Dorothy's interest in Carmen, and suggested strongly that they try to get her the part. They felt she was wrong for it, that she didn't have the fire necessary for it and they were recommending another MCA client singer, Joyce

Bryant, who they felt was a better choice.

This I had to tell Dorothy. It made her even more depressed. MCA had talked to Preminger and he had agreed that Joyce was a better choice.

Preminger came to see Dorothy at La Vie En Rose. His comment was, "She's lovely at La Vie En Rose. A marvelous entertainer. A sophisticated girl but I can't see her in a parachute factory or a sleazy Chicago hotel room with an AWOL soldier."

Dorothy told me she knew that Lena Horne was being tested for the role. However, this didn't bother her as much as other testings. Lena was a big star and it would at least be something acceptable if Lena got the role. But down deep she wanted nobody to have the role but herself.

Each day we would look at the trade papers and see someone else tested. It was like driving a stake into Dorothy's heart. She was stewing in her juices and not knowing what to do about it.

Dorothy asked me to try to arrange an interview with Preminger but I had tried and he refused to see her. He repeated that he thought she was marvelous but not for this role.

Dottie felt that if she could see Preminger she could convince him.

I thought I'd use another tactic. I had offices at 214 South Beverly Drive and in the same building Otto Preminger's brother Ingo had an agency. Obviously I felt if I could convince Ingo, maybe he'd go to his brother and at least get Preminger to grant an interview.

I brought Dorothy's clippings, which were considerable, many magazine articles and some beautiful color pictures of her to Ingo and asked—pleaded—that he try to get Dorothy an interview with Otto. I knew how very important it was for her and for her future.

Two days passed and then a phone call from Preminger saying he would at least see Dorothy. She was hysterical with joy, though I tried to calm her down and told her he was only seeing her and, in fact, when he agreed to see her stated that he didn't think she was right for the part.

He repeated that his concept of Carmen was earthy, provocative, full of excitement and, most important, full of anger, not sophisticated the way Dorothy was. "She's too much like Loretta Young," Otto stated to me. However, Preminger pointed out that he had another role unfilled. That of Joe's first and loyal lost love, Cindy. "A sweet yielding girl," which was the way he pictured Dorothy.

He suggested that Dorothy read the script, spend some time studying the scenes, particularly where Cindy appeared, and then come in for the meeting.

When we met with Otto Preminger it was all polite small talk followed by suggestions of the Cindy role. Dorothy was very disappointed. She and I repeated several times that she wasn't interested in a minor role. I must say Dorothy had courage—the courage of conviction. She believed she was right for Carmen and she wouldn't consider anything else.

Preminger only sat there and smiled. He apparently liked her. He even wanted to help her. Again he said, "Read the script. Study it and then call me when you know the part of Cindy." Otto thought we were dismissed, that would end the meeting.

I never saw Dorothy so angry. "Mr. Preminger, I can play a whore. I'm an actress. I can play a whore as well as I can play a nun. If I could only convince you. I'm not a Cindy. I have much more to me than a Cindy. You don't know what I've gone through."

She rambled on and on. Excited, unhappy, angry. I suggested we take the script and leave. Otto Preminger's opinion of Dorothy Dandridge convinced me producers judge an actress according to how they look and speak. Dorothy was the image of elegance and refinement. She had fitted into the image very nicely and now she asked people to believe she wasn't that way. That she was something else. It wasn't easy to do that. I suggested to Dorothy and Otto that we take the script and come back another time prepared to do scenes for him. At least this would give us another chance to meet with Otto. I told Dorothy my reaction to the meeting. We decided to look like Carmen the next time. We went to Max Factor's and she borrowed a full-length messy-looking black wig, the kind she believed Carmen would wear. Then she put on an off-the-shoulder, low-cut, black peasant blouse without a bra, a black satin skirt with a slit to the thigh without a girdle, and black high-heeled pumps. Then she was made up in the sexy tradition. Even Dorothy was surprised and awed when she saw herself in the mirrors. She felt she might not get the role of Carmen but she was sure as hell certain that she wouldn't be asked to do the role of Cindy.

We had that second meeting with Otto Preminger and Dorothy was determined to let her personality fit her clothes. She swayed her hips as she walked.

When we came in the office Preminger was standing there, an awesome figure, looking toward the door. He took one look at Dorothy in her makeup and get-up and watched her walk and said, dramatically, "My God. You are really Carmen."

Dorothy walked around the room the way she imagined Carmen Jones would walk and Preminger just stood there with his hands on his hips and his lips pouting.

He kept repeating over and over, "It is remarkable," in that thick German accent of his. He didn't say anything to us. He just picked up the phone and made arrangements for a screen test.

We had one foot in the door. There was no holding Dorothy now when we exited the office. She was saying loudly, so that people were looking, "I've got it. I've got it. I know I have it."

They made three movies together and while they got along well in the beginning of the shooting of *Carmen Jones,* Dorothy was soon Otto Preminger's "girl friend" and whatever had been with Harry Belafonte, ended if there ever was a romance in *Bright Road* as rumored.

But I knew she was a long way from having it.

There was a minor problem. Dorothy had scheduled an engagement at the St. Louis Chase Hotel. Preminger thought she should keep the engagement as entertainers get into powerful trouble when they break such an engagement, and he'd defer the test until she finished on May 10th. She had two weeks' stay there. He promised that not only would she take a test but he'd work beforehand with her on the scenes that he thought she should do. These were key scenes that would tell whether she could or could not handle the part.

So Dorothy went to St. Louis for her night club engagement opening May 2, 1952. The Chase Hotel had never engaged a Negro performer before for their elegant dining room. Dorothy would not accept the engagement at the Chase Hotel unless she lived in the hotel as well as her black maid and accompanist. This was arranged by me.

After Dorothy arrived at the Chase and she registered without incident, she received a phone call from the head of NAACP reporting that the Chase Hotel did not allow Negroes to enter their hotel through the front door and only employees were welcome if they were Negroes. They were not served in any of the hotel's restaurants.

Dorothy asked them why they hadn't done anything about this condition in their home town and why they waited until a Negro entertainer was in town and they asked that person to act against prejudice. Dorothy wanted to act on this terrible prejudice and she did. She told the management she would not open her engagement unless Negroes could come to see her show and that they could get reservations and be served. She also wanted Negroes to be allowed to enter through the main entrance, not in the rear delivery entrance.

All the above conditions were agreed to by the

hotel and a table of Negro members of NAACP were in the dining room for her opening show. Dorothy entertained them in her suite at the hotel after her appearance. A liberal Caucasian attorney, a native of St. Louis, who telephone Dorothy on her arrival helped her in accomplishing her wishes. Dorothy appreciated his help and Dorothy and the attorney became good friends. Dorothy enjoyed his company and they saw each other socially and remained friends for years.

Preminger phoned her frequently about the *Carmen* test scenes following her opening.

I'll say this for Preminger, he was meticulous in everything he did, including the test. He partnered her with black actor James Edwards, who had just received critical acclaim for the movie *Home of the Brave*. Edwards was not going into *Carmen* but Preminger wanted him to do the part with Dorothy that Belafonte would do on screen.

The scene chosen was one in which Carmen and Joe are on the run. Joe is AWOL, parted forever from the gentle Cindy, and Carmen is beginning to get unhappy with the fugitive life of poverty. As the scene begins she was alternately sweet and sardonic and doing her toenails in a very sexy camera angle.

Dorothy, for the scene, wore a very brief polka-dot robe with her legs bare. It was a very sensual scene. Especially when Joe, at Carmen's behest, blew on her toenails to make them dry faster. I watched Preminger all during the scene. He was poker-faced but bent over closer to the action when Joe blew on the drying nail polish.

When Joe started kissing Carmen's ankles and her legs and with an odd smile on her face she slid off the kitchen table into his arms, Preminger gave one clap of his hands and smiled.

Further on, Dorothy slowly and provocatively pulled on her stockings while she listened to Joe's pleas not to leave him. It was a good scene. Probably bulletproof for someone like Dorothy with the natural fire in her. It had a lot of emotional, sexual excitement and I'll say that Dorothy did it as well as anyone in the world could have done it. She was full of herself and full of sex.

It was a long test, a grueling one. There wasn't a mistake made by Dorothy and, in all fairness, I have to add that every bit of support that could possibly be given an actress was given by Preminger. He treated the test as if it were an important scene in an important movie. He couldn't have given her more.

At the end of the test, Dorothy just lay back on a couch and there was silence. It was a very dramatic moment. Preminger walked over to her and he said, "Well, young lady, you've got the part. You are Carmen."

She just closed her eyes and put her head back and that's all there was to it. His staff was elated. I think they were as happy as anybody.

The shooting schedule was programmed for ten weeks, beginning June 16th. The original plans were to shoot on location in Florida but then they felt they could find all the exteriors they needed right in California.

If you don't know actresses, the following might be puzzling to you. One day before the first day of shooting, Dorothy called me. Very simply and without a lot of emotion, she said, "Earl, I've decided that I'm not going to do Carmen."

I thought at first it was a joke. But she said, no, she had been to Dr. Berman, her psychiatrist, and she told him that she had proved she could get the role and it wasn't necessary to actually do it. She felt it would complicate her life a great deal and it would cause a lot of extra pressure.

Now I knew I had a fight ahead of me. For twenty-four hours, with her psychiatrist in attendance who wanted her to do the role, through meals and shopping and resting and talking I tried to convince her that she had to do the part. Dorothy was very mixed up by her own admission, so disturbed she couldn't think. I kept coming up with positive answers for every negative excuse. If she wanted a career very badly, this was the greatest opportunity she'd ever have; that acting was her principal interest and Carmen was one of the best roles an actress could portray; that the screen test proved she had the ability to be great in the role.

I wondered how self-destructive she really was, what her guilts and problems were. Why she felt she had to harm herself by walking out on this film, the opportunity of a lifetime. Psychiatry seemed to help only a little, her problems were very deeply rooted. She was on the brink of disaster before every success. She often said to me, "Earl, dear, thank God you're so patient and understanding. I don't know what I'd do without you."

I kept wondering what made this girl so complicated. Every career decision was so difficult for her to make. It was yes and no every time. She's so insecure, I thought. I also knew this is the way most stars and talented people are. One really has to be capable of a labor of love to help talent succeed to the top.

Dorothy had reasons. She said she had a lack of dramatic experience. She didn't want the whole picture to depend on her. She only wanted to prove she could get the role.

None of her successes or reviews helped her confidence. *Carmen* was a major motion picture and one in which she'd have to carry the title role. There wasn't a scene in the script that she wasn't in and she said she was frightened. So why do the role at all? She was panicky.

She had a hundred negative arguments and I had to find a positive one to fit each. I tried to tell her that she had the advantage of an excellent director, Preminger, who had the dual talent of producing and direction, and I pointed out that he believed she could do the role. He had confidence in her and she had given him that confidence. I also pointed out that with Belafonte and Pearl Bailey along with a great cast, she could count on their support and that it still takes a successful Hollywood film to make anyone a big star.

She said, "No," she wouldn't do it.

We were getting close to camera time and still she was saying no, she wouldn't do the role.

Harry Belafonte and Dorothy Dandridge in one of the early confrontations in *Carmen Jones*. Joe (Belafonte) has left his "nice" girlfriend for the provocative Carmen (Dorothy Dandridge).

Pearl Bailey, shown here with Redd Foxx, was the first actor cast for Carmen Jones by Otto Preminger. She played Carmen's girl friend, Frankie, "who lived off the fat of the land and sang "Beat Out That Rhythm On The Drums" in the film. Actually Dorothy Dandridge was the last principal cast.

CHAPTER ELEVEN

On the first morning of shooting *Carmen Jones*, Dorothy was scheduled to leave her house at 5:30 a.m. for make-up. When I drove over to pick her up I did not know if she'd be ready or not. We had talked until 3:00 a.m. by phone. I had no idea even if she'd be home or whether she'd just say, "I won't do it."

So driving through a darkish dawn with virtually no traffic about should have been relaxing, yet, I never felt worse. This was Dorothy's biggest opportunity and she was so frightened it was doubtful whether she would do it.

I parked outside her house, hoping for the best and fearing the worst. The silence was ominous. A stray cat played with an empty beer can in the street. The streets were desolate under a leaden sky.

Then Dorothy came out of the house jaunty and smiling. "Hi," she said happily, as if this wasn't a crisis and as if she had always intended on doing the film.

"To the studio," she said, "and wish me luck." She was all smiles. "You know how I am," she said.

I kissed her on the cheek and kept my mouth shut until we reached the studio. I wished her luck and breathed a sigh of relief.

We didn't know it then but she was undertaking the most important career event of her life. She was on the high curve of her life. For a time she was to be gloriously happy, become an international screen star and have a love affair with Otto Preminger, one of the great directors of Hollywood.

For a time it appeared that Dorothy would go up and up. I believed it and she believed it.

The picture was scheduled to shoot for ten weeks. It was a demanding and exhausting period. Dorothy never faltered. She gave it everything she had, and that was plenty.

She was up every day at five a.m. and often worked until midnight. Preminger was a glutton for hard work and when making a picture was a merciless driver. Dorothy took all he could give and then some. He was tough and determined and she was anxious to make a good picture so she followed every direction meticulously.

She was surprisingly adept at taking instructions. Even the hard-boiled Preminger, who always determined each move of every actor and actress who worked for him, gave her no criticism, except his constant cry to "slow down." He felt Carmen would never hurry, always be assured.

The picture was being filmed in Cinemascope and therefore every gesture would be exaggerated. It was his contention that quick movement would lend insecurity to the total character. That, he didn't want.

Otto exerted a Svengali influence on Dorothy. Like a psychiatrist, he dug her out of herself. She depended upon him for approval. He was her personal God. When he was happy, she was happy, and when he was morose, she was morose.

I watched all this happening and was glad. It was important she have such rapport with her director. They were a team. Together they'd make a good picture.

There was something satanic about Preminger in his zeal for success. There was no compromise ever with him—everything had to be done his way and exactly when he wanted it.

Every day the two of them would go to a small projection room at Twentieth Century Fox and look at the previous day's rushes. Preminger's reaction would decide whether Dorothy's next few hours would be happy or miserable.

After each length of film Preminger would sit and discuss what Dorothy had done and how it could be improved upon, sometimes in detail that no one else would notice. Sometimes, but rarely, Preminger would be happy. Then Dorothy was ecstatic. She had tossed her whole life into Carmen. She lived and breathed it.It had been decided that Dorothy and Belafonte would not sing the opera arias in the Bizet score. It was felt—and she agreed—her voice wasn't right for it. She said she thought several months of intensive practice would make her fit for the role. But there wasn't that much time.

However, even though she couldn't sing the songs, she had to look as if she could. She studied daily an hour or so with Florence Russell, an operatic voice teacher who helped her considerably.

She studied the lip and throat movements of an opera singer and imitated them. After each day's shooting she would get the demos, discs with the songs recorded, and rehearse them with Marilyn Horne, who sang them so beautifully when she recorded them for the film.

Then she'd take the demos home and work through the night, working out the gestures, the physical action, and then the imitation singing of the songs as well as the dramatic scenes.

I would go about my rounds each evening and if I saw a light in Dorothy's window, as I usually did, I'd drop in on her and almost always found her working.

Then still full of energy and excitement, she'd explain the action and the songs. Then she'd go through the movements of Carmen as she'd do it the next day.

Dorothy was becoming as meticulous as Otto Preminger.

It was inevitable that a beautiful woman and a forceful man in proximity day after day should become more than co-workers, more than friends. Yet Hollywood of the early fifties—social Hollywood— wasn't yet ready for a white man and a black woman relationship.

This was a romance that had to be conducted mostly behind closed doors. It seems ridiculous in these enlightened times, but it was apparent in those days that such a combination could cause nothing but trouble in both the studio executive ranks and with the moving going public.

Preminger seemed to be what Dorothy wanted—a man of power and strength who was meaningful in the entertainment world. For him she was a lovely woman with a magnetic sex appeal.

On the set of *Carmen Jones* a gay young bachelor showed Dorothy a card from a madam. It quoted prices thus: Whites $50; Orientals $75; and Negroes $100. The bachelor thought Dorothy would be shocked about that. But instead she showed the card to everyone. It was interesting that a madam thought black girls twice as desirable as whites.

Months later Preminger helped her buy a beautiful home and lavished many gifts on her. Marriage was some vague possibility that might or might not happen. Still marriage was what Dorothy wanted above all else. It didn't happen. Whether Preminger ever seriously considered marrying her was locked in his mind. Maybe yes and maybe no. She loved him and hoped he would. He didn't.

In the beginning and occasionally thereafter, Otto exerted a Svengali influence on Dorothy. He took it upon himself to introduce her into the strata of culture theretofore unknown to her.

He bought her fine art, a star's collection of lingerie, good clothing and antiques. He taught her how to fix a gourmet dinner.

During *Carmen* when the romance first began, she told herself she was going into the relationship with her eyes wide open.

"That's the way it is in Hollywood. You have romance with your director or producer during the making of the film and when the film is over, you go your separate ways."

She made it seem light and casual. This was her defense in case the affair ended suddenly. Yet the romance lasted several years.

Otto was separated from his wife at the time, but not divorced. His wife was openly seen with Michael Rennie, whom Dottie once dated. For that and other reasons, Otto preferred not being seen in public with Dorothy.

She felt the same way. She was uneasy at functions and preferred spending time with Otto at home and away from the movie crowd.

He'd go to his home after a day's shooting and then go to her house for dinner, which she would fix. In the evening he would talk a lot and she was always fascinated with what she heard.

Otto was full of Hollywood lore and he had an interesting way of telling tales of the great and near-greats. She was always complimented by the fact that he would spend so much time with her, certain that she understood his philosophies and his judgment.

When they started having differences of opinion, they jockeyed for position of dominance. At first she was the boss, but soon enough he took over.

A problem was Dorothy's complaint to me about Otto showing up at her night club openings without notice. That would upset her. She liked to sing to an impersonal audience and she was too closely involved with Otto. She didn't want any criticism about her night club work and she was never at her best opening night. She hated saloons.

I remember one time she was due to open in Philadelphia at the Latin Casino. Otto showed up before the opening and they got into an awful fight over his appearance there without warning. She hated openings. Then he didn't like her gown and he had other personal criticism, which precipitated tears. When she finally went on stage she was in no emotional condition to sing.

It was apparent to me immediately that she was on the point of breaking down. Her singing tempo got slower and slower. The audience sensed something was wrong.

I stood there in the wings praying she could last out the song she was singing, but she couldn't. There was a blank look on her face and she stopped singing. She hesitated and collapsed, almost smashing her head on the raised bandstand. I got an ambulance and rushed her to the hospital.

This was all brought on by the emotional conflict with Otto. Otto quickly left town.

Sammy Davis, Jr. was in Philadelphia at the time rehearsing for "Mr. Wonderful" and he kindly filled in for Dorothy until she recovered.

Otto Preminger got so involved in Dorothy's life that he decided he would redo her nightclub act--which had been very successful for years. Dorothy didn't object but the first time he came to see her she became so nervous that she collapsed. He is shown here as a Nazi in the film, *Stalag 17*.

Sammy Davis Jr. with Altovise Davis and Dinah Shore. Having both grown up in show business, Sammy and Dorothy Dandridge were friends since childhood. When Dorothy suffered a physical breakdown during an engagement in Philadelphia, Sammy stepped in and filled in for her a few days.

CHAPTER TWELVE

There came a series of confrontations with Otto Preminger. Otto's hand was constantly in evidence in Dorothy's professional life. Had he been just her lover it would have been better, but he wanted to control every facet of her life.

Once Dorothy excitedly told me Otto was going to help her with her act. One of Hollywood's most distinguished directors would help her fashion her act. She was delighted and pleased. I was a little less than enthusiastic. Night club acts are different from motion pictures.

Dorothy, who was now an international sex symbol, thought of herself as something else. She wanted to be a lady, a nun, on stage. She thought of herself as a patrician lady of elegance. She didn't want to be identified as a sex symbol!

Otto agreed she should change her image. The two of them got their heads together and Dorothy got a new gown, a long black, loose-fitting robe type of costume, and changed her repertoire.

This was the new Dandridge. She opened in Florida with her new image, and the act was an abysmal failure.

She soon went back to the old Dorothy

Dandridge.

To sum it up, Dorothy was happy during most of her long romance with Preminger. He added another dimension to her life. He gave as well as took, which wasn't true of all her other lovers.

Dorothy thought that she and Otto would get married. Near the end of her relationship with Otto, she became friendly with Jack Dennison. In every relationship prior to Otto, each personal friend kept in touch with her which pleased her very much. It was different with Otto. She felt bitter towards him.

She said she was pregnant once but she wouldn't tell me by whom. Having an abortion upset her for a long, long time.

Other than Otto Preminger, during the making of *Carmen*, Dorothy, as she usually did during a film, kept to her dressing room. She was usually either with her secretary or her hairdresser. It took Dorothy a long time to make friends and she looked with suspicion on most new acquaintances.

Dorothy was usually under psychiatric analysis. She needed that as a crutch. Her life was peppered with crises and when these emotional upsets happened, she needed someone to run to. Dr. Jack Berman attended her for years and saw her through one crises after another.

On the set of Carmen, Dorothy made one other friend. That was Pearl Bailey. It wasn't that they talked a lot, but there was warmth between them. Dorothy would say, "You know, I think she likes me."

When Dorothy died, at her bedside was a thank you note to Pearl for a gift set of philosophical books.

When the film was completed, a world premiere was set for the New York Rivoli Theater on October 28, 1954. And while Dorothy continued her career without interruption, it was clear she thought of not much else but the opening of *Carmen*. Preminger was supremely confident but Dorothy was rocked by every sort of doubt. She had nightmares of reading bad reviews and dreams of wild acclaim. Preminger would have long, quiet talks with her explaining why the film was good. But Dorothy could see a hundred spots in the film where she might have done better.

Just before the premiere the Hollywood trade papers, the Reporter and Variety, reviewed the film and liked it. They enjoyed it critically as well as with an eye to the box office. Just after that, a preview of the picture was held in a small Westwood Village theater. This was important to Dorothy because it was momentous in her life as to how her Negro friends responded to her career moves. If the whole world liked *Carmen* and they did not, it would be a hollow victory.

So with much trepidation Dorothy invited her closest friends to the preview. The theater was also near UCLA, and Dorothy wasn't sure how the college people would react to *Carmen*.

The audience seemed to respond to the drama. It was a lush, opulent screen treatment and the drama and music were excellent. On the other hand, Dorothy's friends didn't seem to react, one way or another. Dorothy didn't know if they liked it or not. She invited everyone to her house for drinks after the preview. She listened to comments but heard nothing.

She thought maybe the image they had of her was too much different from the temptress she played in the movie. To her question: "How did you like it?" they all replied so that their answer could be interpreted in any way. One said, "I liked it but I'd like to think about it for a while."

After they all left Dorothy and I talked about it and couldn't come to any conclusion. She was depressed because of their lack of enthusiasm.

Whatever the reasons, the evening hadn't ended well for Dorothy. She still was full of doubts—even more so than usual. Preminger never lost a beat of optimism. He believed it was a fine movie and would be well received.

The principals went to New York for the premiere. Harry Belafonte was interviewed and said, "It proves there's no corner of human drama that Negroes cannot play. However, I don't think Hollywood as a whole is geared to pioneering of this sort. I say thank God for the independent producer."

Dorothy was happy that Harry felt the picture helped the Negro race. That was always uppermost in her mind. She was always sensitive to what the Negroes would think of her work.

When she was interviewed she only said she hoped the picture was a box office success and that she'd be able to do other pictures. She said she'd like to do one or two pictures a year and settle down in Hollywood without having to continue the grind of nightclub dates on the road.

Dorothy's mother, Ruby, was working and couldn't come to the premiere, but her sister Vivian flew out. She arrived at the premiere beautifully gowned and alone. Her sister and friends were to meet her inside. She was greeted with resounding cheers by the curious crowd. She had just appeared on a prestige all-star, two-hour "Light Diamond Jubilee" TV show with Helen Hayes and others and would go to the Steve Allen Show after the premiere for another TV appearance.

The audience was full of celebrities. Dorothy sat with her sister and was strangely calm. This was the moment she had always waited for, yet she was perfectly relaxed. There was no doubt this was her picture. She was Carmen and everything revolved about her.

Vivian was more nervous than Dorothy. It was strange that within four years, Vivian became a missing person. Detectives were paid a small fortune but Vivian never saw her sister alive again. It was one more shock to Dorothy.

Vivian Dandridge reappeared in New York, where

she now lives, after having dropped from sight until 1969.

But this evening, Vivian supplied moral support. From the "Wonder Children" to oblivion was her story. Later Dorothy would talk about fate and how she and her sister, as the "Wonder Children," had hopes of conquering the world.

The picture had three things going for Dorothy. It was a black movie with a great starring role. She was beautiful and talented. And *Carmen* was a famous story bordering on the classic with great music beautifully performed in Cinemascope and magnificent color.

The audience interrupted the film several times with applause. At the end of the film there was a standing ovation. Dorothy cried with joy.

The reviews were excellent. Dorothy was elated. Life magazine carried a picture of Dorothy on its cover, the first black to break the color barrier at Life. The review inside said, "She succeeds brilliantly in the straight dramatic role of the rose-toting wanton who tempts an honest soldier into deserting and then jilts him."

Newsweek and Time Magazines had paeans of praise for her. She bathed in the warmth of love. Preminger was full of "I-told-you-so's." And he was right.

The picture was a smash at the box office. She was happy to leave New York and make a series of personal appearances to coincide with the opening of the film in different cities. Dorothy had one need—that this film be a smash success. It was.

By 1958, the picture would make a profit of three million dollars. It would be shown at the Cannes Film Festival in a special non-competitive screening, but it has never been seen in any other French theater. Invoking the Convention of Geneva of 1902, Bizet's publishers, M. Choudens of Paris, while admitting that non-signatories to the convention (by which they meant every country except France) might use the opera *Carmen* as they saw fit, they would not permit what they called "the criminal story to be distorted" and distributed in France.

Otto Preminger made a special trip to Europe in an attempt to persuade Choudens to change their minds, but he failed.

In Munich, *Carmen Jones*, with German subtitles, ran for almost two years, and won a citation for the longest run in the theater's history.

It drew the ire of Pravda, which reported in what seems anger and astonishment: "The entire dramatis personae consists of Negroes." Somehow it discovered that, "We see before us the standard crime and American comics in music. How can such cheap trash be combined with the deep artistic and realistic music of Bizet?"

It also ran into trouble in Tupelo, Mississippi, where on January 31, 1955, Guy Repolt, spokesman for the Tupelo Moose Lodge, demanded city officials show *Carmen Jones* in Negro theaters only. Reflecting an apparent discontent with Hollywood product in general, Repolt threw down the gauntlet yet again by stating:" and we don't want *Barefoot Contessa* shown at all in our city."

The success of *Carmen* gained Dorothy Dandridge a three-year contract at Twentieth Century, signed February 15, 1955, which was the first and most ambitious ever offered to a black performer. Darryl F. Zanuck and his studio promised her three pictures, one each year with a salary escalating from $75,000 to $125,000 per film. The contract was non-exclusive, giving her freedom to do outside pictures, and then in almost an unprecedented move, Zanuck gave his star "Billing above the Title." Dorothy had become the first Negro international film star in the history of motion pictures.

Dorothy Dandridge with Pierre Salinger in New York. Salinger had attended a club date by the singer as he was a loyal fan. Interestingly, the little girl from the Wonder Children went a long way in her career and became friends with dozens of rich and famous people.

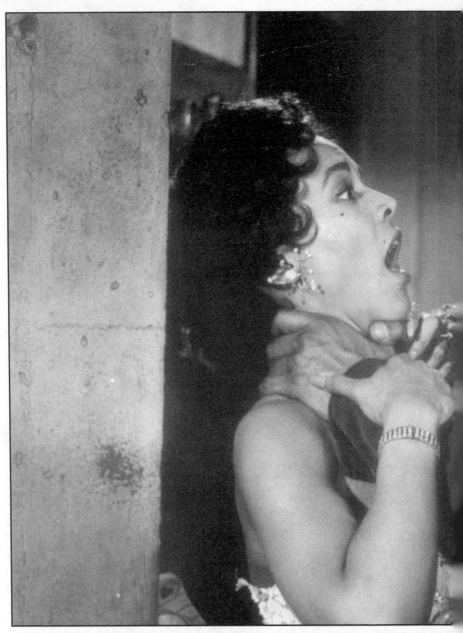

The principals went to New York for the premiere of *Carmen*. Harry Belafonte was interviewed and said, "It proves there's no corner of human drama that Negroes cannot play. However, I don't think Hollywood as a whole is geared to pioneering of this sort. I say thank God for the independent producer."

Dorothy was happy that Harry felt the picture helped the Negro race, always a subject dear to her. She was ever sensitive to what the Negroes would think of her work. When she was interviewed she only said she hoped the picture was a box office success and that she'd be able to do other pictures.

Dorothy Dandridge in a scene from the Twentieth Century-Fox production of
Island In The Sun the first interracial love story produced in Hollywood. It also
starred James Mason, Joan Fontaine, Harry Belafonte, Joan Collins and Michael
Rennie and was well received by movie fans.

CHAPTER THIRTEEN

Dorothy gained a 1955 Academy Award nomination as the best actress of the year for *Carmen Jones*. No Negro had ever been honored as a film star this way even though Hattie McDaniel won an award for the best supporting actress for *Gone With The Wind* in 1940.

It led immediately to the Empire Room of the Waldorf-Astoria Hotel and a seven—week stay. It was a first for a Negro entertainer.

Singing at the Empire Room at the Waldorf-Astoria was fun. She was at the peak of her career. Talented Nick Perito very successfully wrote great music arrangements for her. He became her conductor-pianist and staunch friend for many years. Yet she was not happy for very long. Dorothy had never been happy when there was no love in her life. And love is nothing that can be manufactured, so there was nothing, nothing at all that I could do about it.

I was getting worried about her. All she did was rehearse, exercise and sleep. Even her shopping excursions which she had enjoyed had been curtailed.

In those days it was fashionable to get vitamin shots and I convinced Dorothy to go to a doctor and get some shots. She had the hotel doctor come in. I felt the electricity between them while he was examining her.

After some preliminaries he asked politely if I'd please leave the room. The only reason I had stayed was because Dorothy asked me to. But I retreated. I could hear him through the double doors say, "There's nothing wrong with you that plenty of applause wouldn't cure." He was wrong there. She had plenty of applause each night but she was still dragging her heels.

He casually said after giving her a vitamin shot, "I'll stop in tomorrow to see how you are. About this time, all right?"

It was all right.

On the following Sunday he took her to see some old films at the Metropolitan Museum. She had always liked that. His name was Bret and they dug each other from the start.

It was a shot in the arm for her in double dose. She immediately perked up and even her performances had more zip. Soon she told me, "Doctor Bret is odd. Sometimes he's so charming and outgoing and other times he's moody and inhibited. It's as if he were two separate men."

I found that not so confounding. I knew other men who were that way. She said she couldn't quite explain it but his case was different. We found out he was a rather famous doctor and treated many celebrities. He was known on both coasts.

Then Dorothy solved part of the mystery. The good doctor was on some kind of pill that we now call "happy" pills. When he didn't have the "up" pill he got very depressed. The fact is he had been taking both "up" and sedative pills like Seconal and they kept him on a see-saw.

That's all Dorothy had to hear. She liked to rehabilitate people and especially someone worthwhile like a doctor. In short time, she was the doctor and he was the patient. She had a knack for instilling great confidence in herself. Others relied on it. Soon she was slipping him placebos (sugar pills) instead of the real thing and he was regaining his equilibrium.

When it was time for her to return to Hollywood he was completely normal again. Dorothy was often a remarkable woman.

Soon after she got back she told me, "The doctor was almost impotent from drugs when I first met him. That's why his wife left him. Now he is virile again."

I asked her, "But did he help you?"

Her answer was a shrug. Dorothy enjoyed helping others.

The first of the films on her new contract was to be *Island In The Sun*. It was to star James Mason, Joan Fontaine, Harry Belafonte, Joan Collins and Michael Rennie, along with Dorothy Dandridge. The property was engineered for purchase by Darryl Zanuck because he could envision it getting the same kind of fine critical comment and good box office that *Gentleman's Agreement* did. That one was a well-done plea for religious tolerance while *Island In The Sun*, which was a best-selling book, was a plea for racial tolerance. It was to portray the first interracial romance in the history of motion pictures by a major film producer.

Zanuck was the first to tackle this subject which was then dynamite. In fact, he was a little too soon because with no rules to govern how far the story could go on celluloid, there was constant confusion in the ranks.

At the time, I discussed it in detail with Dorothy and we came to the same conclusion. The Caucasian-Negro problem in this film was handled with all the problems and confusion that existed in real life. Darryl Zanuck tried hard to compromise with all points of view. The book had a dignified romance between Dorothy and the British actor John Justin.

To better understand why the problems of the film appeared to loom larger than they really were to

Dorothy, we have to go back to her Riviera engagement in Las Vegas (at $20,000 a week). Sell-out crowds were delighted with her and Dorothy was happy in the room.

The maitre-d' was a handsome, graying man named Jack Dennison who had all the smoothness and charm of any head waiter in an important hotel. He took to sending Dorothy nightly arrangements of flowers and gratis servings of good food always attended by several waiters anxious to please her.

Dorothy almost accepted this as her due, so Dennison didn't get much of a reaction. But he persisted with his attentions and on her closing night he showed up with the figures relating how marvelously she had done during her stay. He told her sadly of the one big love in his life with another Negro girl and how they had planned to marry, but she died. (The truth, as told to Dorothy later on, was that the black girl was pregnant with Dennison's child and died soon after a baby girl was born. A group of prominent Negroes, including Joe Louis, contributed to bringing her up when Dennison failed to provide support for her.)

The magic word that Dennison spoke was "marriage." He intentionally, or maybe unintentionally, dangled the word marriage as bait before a girl on the rebound from her romance with Otto Preminger. He slowly was about to get his hooks into her.

When she came back to Los Angeles, he called her every day and flew in on his days off. They became friends and then lovers.

Then came *Island In The Sun*. She had to leave her lover to go on location in Jamaica.

That was the mood Dorothy was in at the start of *Island In The Sun*. She kept in daily touch with Dennison by telephone which wasn't easy. From the islands she had to make daily reservations at the post office to be sure of getting a phone line to the States. The two had constant misunderstandings on the long distance phone. It was a poor way for love to flourish.

Then the constant problem in the making of the film was how far black and white could go on the screen in their lovemaking. For example, the director didn't know about John Justin, a white British actor saying "I love you" to Dorothy. He changed the line to, "You know how I feel." There were many problems such as that. Dorothy was nettled by all of them.

She could identify now with her own romance with Jack Dennison and it bothered her. That was one big problem and there was still another. As is customary on film locations, most of the principals had teamed up in couples—that is, all except Harry Belafonte and Dorothy. He liked her but she wouldn't play. After all, she had a boy friend whom she loved and she always prided herself on being a one-man woman.

This made Belafonte furious. Once when she wouldn't come out of her room, he broke her door and carried her out.

Belafonte told her that the annual limbo contest was to be held by the islanders.

Immediately Dorothy wanted to enter the contest. It sounded like fun and her fellow entertainers were all for it—James Mason, Harry Belafonte, Joan Fontaine and the others. All were uneasy about it because it is practically an athletic event and requires great skill and practice. Not Dorothy. She loved acrobatics and competition.

If you wonder what a limbo contest is, it is simply the ability of contestants to dance leaning progressively backwards under a horizontal bar without falling or touching the bar. The bar is lowered progressively until just the winner is left. It is a little like a high jumping contest, only in this case, the bar is lowered each time.

On the night of the eliminations, contestants came from all over the islands to sign up for the championships.

As the contestants flocked in, James Mason, Harry

Harry Belafonte and Joan Fontaine in *Island In The Sun*. The Caucasian-Negro problem in this film was handled with all the problems and confusion that existed in real life. Darryl Zanuck tried hard to compromise with all points of view. The book contained a dignified romance between Dorothy and the British

actor John Justin. However, in Dandridge's mind it wasn't filmed that way:
"What my character has turned out to be is a whore. I'm always sitting on a
brass bed with my stockings down." Dorothy's opinion was black actresses were
to often treated this way. Nevertheless, the film was a success.

Belafonte and Joan Fontaine became more and more alarmed. They took their limbo contests seriously here. Large prizes were awarded and winners were admired just like football and baseball champions in the States.

Because of her exercising and dancing, Dorothy was in excellent condition. Dorothy was also slim, which gave her an advantage.

Music started and soon the fat, the clumsy, the clowns and the uninitiated were eliminated. Dorothy, full of grace, made the early minutes of the game seem easy.

Soon laughter subsided and the competition became serious. It wasn't long before the past champions and Dorothy were left to compete in the final round. The circle of onlookers was hushed. The night was still. The music started again and one ex-champion toppled the limbo stick with a foolish move sideways.

Soon only Sophia Hernandez, the past season's champion, and Dorothy were left. They hugged before starting the last round just as boxers would shake hands. Lower and lower went the stick until it looked impossible to go under it. Sophia danced under and knocked the stick off. "Oohs" went up from the crowd. Could Dorothy get under the same height? The crowd was hushed. The music struck up again. Dorothy danced and wiggled and she made it. It was one of the happiest moments of her life.

She would go swimming with James Mason and take dramatic lessons from him, but it was just a friendship.

At one point Belafonte became so frustrated and angry he sent for Julie Robinson, a white girl he liked, who was a former Katherine Dunham dancer. She flew in to keep him company. He later married her, a marriage that, from all appearences, has been very successful and happy. The chances are, Dorothy's behavior led to the marriage.

About this time, Dorothy was so upset she phoned me and begged me to get her off the film for a while. She just had to see Dennison and get everything straightened out. He was to meet her in New York.

Because *Island In The Sun* had to be finished in London (the weather in Jamaica was terrible), Zanuck gave Dorothy permission to leave the company for a while. She flew to New York where Dennison met her.

Dorothy phoned me about what was happening to the picture: "What my character has turned out to be is a whore. I'm always sitting on a brass bed with my stockings down. It's so hard for them to think of a Negro island girl as anything but a prostitute." She spoke heatedly about it. Nevertheless, the film was a courageous first step by Zanuck and a box office success.

In New York, Dorothy and Dennison had numerous arguments over trivial things like the gloves she bought and what hotel to stay at and what to eat. In a moment of sanity, they decided to take the long trip back to Los Angeles to see if they could find some peace. The rocky part of their romance had started and eventually ended in disaster.

In the newspapers, Dorothy Dandridge was a great star, but in reality, her life was becoming miserable with only occasional triumphs.

Dorothy finished *Island In The Sun* in London and it became apparent what Dorothy's cinematic problem would be. A male Negro like Sidney Poitier could become a big star without romantic roles. But a Dorothy Dandridge had to sizzle on screen. She was a romantic leading lady. But the public wasn't ready for a black woman in that role yet.

Zanuck and other movie brass, realizing the possible potency of a Dorothy Dandridge at the box office, sent story heads scurrying to find a story to fit her. It wasn't easy within the boundaries of the conventions of those days.

As nothing concrete came along, I looked around Europe for her. Their conventions weren't as tight. I put together a picture titled *Tamango* (still on late TV) with the Austrian star, Curt Jurgens. There was no opposition to love scenes between the blonde, blue-eyed Curt and the brown Dorothy for the European market. She got $125,000 for the film plus $500 a week living expenses, her own hairdresser at studio expense, a chauffeured limousine for the twelve weeks she was on the film. She was one of the most popular of all American stars in Europe.

In *Tamango* Dorothy played an African slave, half Negro, half white, loved by a white ship captain, Jurgens. For intimate love scenes there were two versions made. One was for release in the States and one everywhere else. Major distributors screened the film and blinked. The unwritten rule of the Motion Picture Producers Association did not approve of any intimacy or physical contact between black and white.

So while the film turned out fine, it had little exposure in this country.

Soon after that with Dorothy's career still booming, she was chosen for another foreign native role in *The Decks Ran Red,* co-starring James Mason and Stuart Whitman. She got $75,000 for this picture. There nearly was a love scene in it with Stuart Whitman. *Carmen Jones* was still her number one hit by far. Neither Dorothy nor I could find a role in which she could portray an American girl. In all her films she was a foreign native girl unless it was an all-Negro film in which she had to be a near prostitute or on drugs.

Behind the scenes something was happening that probably contributed to the fact that Dorothy couldn't find film roles. Hollywood has always been known for its great promotion genius. Unknowns have been catapulted to stardom by an avalanche of press—newspaper and magazine publicity. But the brass in Hollywood were puzzled as to how to publicize a

Earl Mills put together a picture titled *Tamango* (still on late TV) with the Austrian star, Curt Jurgens. There was no opposition to love scenes between the blue-eyed Curt and the brown Dorothy for the European market. She got $125,000 for the film plus $500 a week living expenses.

Negro. The Negro star needs this attention the same as any other actor, thereby contributing to a big box office gross, but on the other hand, there was fear of antagonizing that portion of the audience that objected to black actors, and therefore hurt the box office.

In 1955, this was a constant problem because of race prejudice, so they more or less sat on their hands and Dorothy was given very little typical film star publicity.

Actually Dorothy had many years of continuous frustration as an actress, even though she was a star. Also the pictures that she starred in handled the problems of race like they'd handle delicate egg shells. For instance, in 1959, a film called *Malaga* starred Dorothy and Trevor Howard. The script was rather vague as to what Dorothy's nationality was supposed to be. When the problem arose as to when or where Trevor Howard should kiss Dorothy, the brass decided there should be no kiss. It was very frustrating to Dorothy and to her friends—and to Trevor Howard.

As these things happened, scripts were changed for the worse each day and there were long writers' conferences. Despite Dorothy's and my assertion that people would accept an honest black-white relationship, no one on the executive level was quite sure and would not take the chance.

About this time Dorothy was still seeing Otto Preminger from time to time. Her romance with Dennison was going very strong and she was also seeing her longtime dear friend Peter Lawford. Her two biggest and contrasting Hollywood romances, Peter Lawford and Otto Preminger, were cultured men, interested in the arts and the better things in life. Peter Lawford remained always her friend.

Dorothy was always magnetized by cultured men in her quest for respect. How Jack Dennison got into the picture, I don't know. His appeal to her must have been his good looks and what appeared to be good manners.

A male such as Sidney Poitier could become a big star without romantic roles. But a Dorothy Dandridge had to sizzle on screen. She was a romantic leading lady. However the public wasn't ready for a black woman in that role yet, just as it had not been for Lena Horne a decade earlier.

Samuel Goldwyn was going to produce *Porgy and Bess* and he wanted Dorothy as Bess. The Negro organizations created a controversy about Hollywood only making all-Negro "undignified" films. A mysterious fire burned down all the movie's sets just prior to the start of the film. Belafonte and others refused roles in the film. Preminger was criticized for being prejudiced. Mr. Goldwyn considered the famous musical an honest historic portrayal of blacks.

The controversial *Porgy and Bess* was finally made, starring Dorothy, Sidney Poitier, Sammy Davis, Jr., Diahann Caroll, Pearl Bailey and others. In fact, for her performance as Bess, Dorothy won a Golden Globe Award of Merit for Outstanding Achievement for the Best Performance by an Actress, awarded by the Hollywood Foreign Press Association. Her spirits were lifted up again, once more, to the heights as a movie star. It gave her new hope. But from that point, it was to be downhill, personally and in her career.

Dorothy thought after *Porgy and Bess* she would be deluged with picture offers. None came.

Dorothy thought that Cleopatra might be made with a Negro girl, such as she. Rouben Mamoulian was going to direct the picture and he lunched with Dorothy at Romanoff's. He told her he thought she'd be perfect for the part but by this time Dorothy had learned plenty.

She said, "They'd never let you get away with it. They'll talk you out of it. It would take too much guts to use a Negro in the part." In the end, she was right.

Jack Dennison pursued her constantly during her frustrations while filming *Malaga* in London. She finally said yes.

It was a surprise to everyone because in the columns she was linked to Peter Lawford, Otto Preminger and others in the film industry. Everyone thought Dorothy would marry a prominent person with dignity, wealth and national importance. It wasn't

Jack Dennison pursued her constantly during her frustrations while filming *Malaga* in London. She finally said yes. It was a surprise to everyone because in the columns she was linked to Peter Lawford, Otto Preminger and others in the film industry. Dennison would ruin her financially.

The controversial *Porgy and Bess* was finally made, starring Dorothy, Sidney Poitier, Sammy Davis, Jr., Diahann Caroll, Pearl Bailey and others. In fact, for her performance as Bess, Dorothy won a Golden Globe Award of Merit for Outstanding Achievement for the

Best Performance by an actressawarded by the Hollywood Foreign Press Association. Her spirits were lifted up again, once more, to the heights as a movie star. It gave her new hope. But from that point, it was to be downhill, personally and in her career.

to be. They were married at a Greek Orthodox church, followed by a dinner party at Tracton's Restaurant (where Dorothy fell asleep). They later went to Dennison's restaurant on Sunset Boulevard for publicity and promotion.

Dennison and others took over management of her career. She was happy in the beginning. This was something she had always wanted. To be married to a handsome man who could support her and keep her off the road while she pursued good film roles. After all, she had a Fox contract!

"Why can't Hollywood put me in the role of an Indian or Mexican girl if they haven't got the guts to do stories about Negroes?" she complained. But so did Indian and Mexican actresses.

She couldn't fight the code, or we might say the "hidden code," and the theater owners that were either prejudiced or concerned about the prejudices of the movie audience.

Another thing that bugged her was that even when she did sit down with a producer to discuss a part, it was always the Carmen image and a girl with no sense of morality. Was this because she was black? She would constantly say, "I'm an actress and I've always worked hard to become a competent one. I interpret a role to the best of my ability. I can do most anything. Why do I always have to play a passionate woman of easy virtue because I'm Negro? I'm not going to do any more roles like that if I can help it."

Despite being married, men she met thought she was like Carmen or over-sexed and they were constantly offering her huge bank accounts to run away with them. As soon as Dennison took over managing her, I got a curt telegram from her saying I wasn't needed anymore as her personal manager. So this union from which she had gone from earning $350 a week to $20,000 weekly and $100,000 per film was suddenly ended after eight years of very hard work .

When she married Jack Dennison Dorothy's career was booming, she was chosen for another foreign native role in *The Decks Ran Red,* co-starring James
Mason and Stuart Whitman. She got $75,000 for the picture but still they were
afraid to let her do a love scene with Whitman as written.

When she divorced Dennison she asked me to come back, and I did. Her marriage to Dennison was a failure in many ways. She made most of the financial contributions and she said he sat by and enjoyed them. He only seemed in the beginning to have a real affection for her. "Everything changed the day we were married," she said.

When she married him she was making $250,000 a year in 1959. She made not one tenth of that at the end, and in 1962 when she filed for divorce, her debts were over $127,000. Her assets were $5,000. The divorce was a bitter one. She charged Dennison with extreme mental cruelty and claimed he had struck her on several occasions. She asked no alimony but she said her husband had mutual debts with her and that the debts were incurred principally for the benefit of the defendant, namely Dennison. She asked that he be required to pay $14,600.

The total amount of financial, emotional and health stress placed on her during the Dennison marriage was so great that it nearly killed her. She was a complete personal wreck when I again assumed management of her career after a three-year period.

The bankruptcy petition listed seventy-seven creditors in all, among them hotels, travel agencies, banks, doctors, utility companies, laundries, pharmacies and supermarkets. It indicated some bad investments and revealed something else—the star's shrinking income.

In 1962, Dorothy earned only $60,000—less than her fee for one motion picture at her peak. In 1963, she grossed $40,000. What a star earns is far from what is taken to the bank. After arrangements, gowns, music and staff are paid for, you realize how very little she did earn.

At this point, her nightclub salary was down to $1,500 a week from $7,500 at her peak. In Las Vegas she had been paid $17,500 weekly.

With a second divorce and the bankruptcy,

Dorothy's confidence deserted her. She was offered few small town nightclub spots and no movies. I was shocked to learn about her very poor health and that her new doctor gave her pills for everything—energy, relaxants, sleeping pills, pills for dehydration, etc.

She had an acute anemic condition, was deeply angry, bitter, hostile, over-sensitive, drinking heavily. She was constantly at the doctor's office, but she didn't quit.

Revitalizing Dorothy's career was a tough job, but I had great affection for her and was determined that she'd work and work in the best spots again.

I reviewed the songs she was singing and reinstated the great audience favorites she was known for: "Blow Out The Candle," "Talk Sweet Talk To Me," "What Is This Thing Called Love," and other songs about happy love. I persuaded Dorothy to leave the doctor who was too eager to give her a pill for everything, and after finding out how bad her health was, we both went to Rancho La Puerto, a marvelous health ranch in Mexico.

At the ranch she ate organic foods, exercised daily, and slept long, peaceful hours. We became lovers. Dorothy told me she "finally had the honeymoon she always wanted." After her ranch experience, Dorothy was again functioning with natural energy, enthusiasm, and her old ambitions to have the Negro community feel proud of her, and a return of success for herself. She wanted to show everybody she could make it big again, even bigger than before. She was sure she soon would win an Academy Award for best actress and be the biggest Negro star ever.

The small town engagements became more and more successful. She starred as Julie in "Showboat" in Burlingame, California, with Kathryn Grayson. This was a role she dreamed of playing on the screen. She was always angry that Hollywood used a Caucasian in the role of a Negro, even though her friend Ava

In *Tamango* Dorothy played an African slave, half Negro, half white, loved by a white ship captain, Jurgens. For intimate love scenes there were two versions filmed. One was for release in the United States and the second released for foreign audiences.

Major distributors screened the film and blinked. The unwritten rule of the Motion Picture Producers Association did not approve of any intimacy or physical contact between black and white. So while the film turned out fine, it had little exposure in The United States.

Gardner performed it extremely well for MGM.

In April, 1965, Dorothy worked in Puerto Rico. The press responded in a manner that pleased her greatly. One newspaper published:

DOROTHY DANDRIDGE IS FULL OF GRACE
by Miguel A Yumet

Puerto Rico Sheraton Hotel, April 3, 1965.

Since I saw her in the movie picture "Carmen Jones" some years ago, I was fascinated by Dorothy Dandridge. The shape is perfect but there is something in that figure when she walks, when she moves, that reminds us of the young panthers. The face has the perfection of a Madonna, but there is something in the depth of her gaze that intrigues and provokes a sleepless (unpeaceful) dream. The mouth is reddish, but there is something in the lips that incites helplessly to a kiss

Some years passed by after the film "Carmen Jones" came to Puerto Rico, and then came Dorothy Dandridge, encircled in the aureola of her name; singing, wrapped up in the glitter that she irradiates. They saw her, yes, on stage, full of beautiful sounds coming from her lofty throat, smiling when receiving the applause.

Now Dorothy Dandridge is preceded by a legend of love. She sings at the Carnival Room of the Hotel Sheraton. She sings better than before and she is more beautiful than ever. It is incredible, that the years, instead of tarnishing this sun-burned rose, have respected its freshness and splendour.

After her debut Saturday night, I could for the first time speak with Dorothy Dandridge at her hotel room. With myself, there were other members of the Press. I never saw a more delicate and softer feminine hand, stretching out with more cordiality. Never before were we greeted by a feminine voice so full of sweetness.

There was no need for asking questions. She talked, talked, and told things about herself with great ease. Although she was wearing a simple but very elegant and rich white evening gown that circled her like a pod, she showed us some of the exercises that help her keep her figure. She pulled her dress up to her knees, and when her beautiful legs were shown, the men almost whistled.

Many men must have gone mad for this woman. Lucky the mortal who can be the owner of her heart. Few times can you find in the world, a woman who can combine such a stupendous beauty with such a vibrating personality and such an artistic and creative talent as Dorothy Dandridge has.

A Tokyo engagement soon followed and Dorothy was now earning $5,000 weekly. Joe Glaser regarded Dorothy as a "daughter" of his; he had managed her twenty-five years earlier when he discovered her in a small Los Angeles ghetto club with the Dandridge Sisters and he arranged the Cotton Club and London tour for the trio. It was Joe Glaser who loaned Dorothy $10,000 after her bankruptcy to get started again.

In June, 1965, Joe Glaser phoned me to tell me he had arranged a wonderful New York appearance for Dorothy at the same location where she became recognized as a top night club attraction ten years earlier, La Vie En Rose, now called Basin Street East.

Dorothy was delighted and she knew now that she was going to make it big again. "I'm going to set New York on their ears," she said. Joe Glaser also got her the Ed Sullivan show, and other television and club engagements to follow.

Four days before the New York opening, a Mexican film producer, Raul Fernandez, phoned me and said he was interested in meeting Dorothy for a film he was producing. He described the role, that of a Mexican peasant girl, and said he was planning a second film about early Mexican history in which he wanted Dorothy to play a native Mexican princess. Dorothy was loved throughout all of Latin America for *Carmen Jones* and *Porgy and Bess*, as well as her personal appearances in Rio, Mexico and pre-Castro Havana, where life-size pictures lined the streets where she was performing.

I arranged a meeting between Dorothy and Raul Fernandez. We flew to Oaxaca, Mexico, to talk with him.

Although her star had slipped somewhat in Hollywood, (there were just no parts for her being offered--or even being found--or perhaps even being looked for) she was still popular as a club singer and she was beginning to explore television. Shown opposite she is doing the Mike Douglas show promoting an engagement at the La Vie En Rose, which was soon renamed Basin Street East. She was booked to open there a few days after her death.

Dorothy, now healthy again, was at her best. She quickly convinced the Mexican producer Fernandez that she was the actress he needed for his two pictures.
Right there she signed a contract for a total fee of $100,000.
Exactly the kind of financial medicine she needed.

CHAPTER FOURTEEN

Dorothy, now healthy again, was at her best. She quickly convinced Fernandez that she was the actress he needed for his two pictures. Right there she signed a contract for a total fee of $100,000. Exactly the kind of financial medicine she needed.

However, the day before leaving for Mexico, on September 3rd, Dorothy turned her ankle while walking down a flight of stairs in a gymnasium and all the time she was in Mexico she complained of it hurting. I got a doctor and he took an X-ray. He said the indication was a broken bone in her ankle. But we were set for a flight back to Los Angeles the next day as we couldn't stay in Mexico any longer.

He bandaged her leg and gave her a crutch to walk on and I arranged for her to see another doctor when we got home.

When we reached L.A. on the 7th, we went to a hospital where Dorothy was attended by her personal physician and an orthopedic specialist. Another X-ray confirmed the bone fracture and Dorothy was asked to come back to the hospital the next morning to have the break set and a cast put on.

She was very upset about it but the doctor told her,

"You'll be able to dance on your feet twenty-four hours after the cast is off." This was all she needed to hear. She was very happy. She was determined again to earn the kind of money she earned once and to prove to all that she was better than ever before. We separated late that evening with the understanding I would pick her up at her apartment at seven-thirty the next morning for her appointment at the hospital.

But at seven-fifteen she phoned me. She said she had been late getting to bed the night before, "doing women's things," talking to her girl friend, companion and maid, Allige Pearon, and getting ready for her New York departure. Also, talking with her mother about all the good news took a lot of time. She wanted to rest longer. She asked me to try and arrange a later appointment for the cast.

I rearranged the appointment for ten a.m., which suited Dorothy, and I phoned and confirmed it. She said, "You know how I am about these things. I'll sleep for a while and I'll be fine." These were her last words.

When I tried to reach her by telephone later I failed to get an answer, so I figured she had decided to sleep through her scheduled hospital appearance. But as it got to be noon, I went to her apartment. She didn't answer the door. I thought she was probably dog-tired and sleeping, so I left.

At two o'clock I felt more confident about going back to the apartment because I knew she was having some gowns delivered by Gladys Williams, her friend and dressmaker. The cleaners were to make a delivery of clothes necessary for New York and Allige Pearon had to get in to start packing the wardrobe for the trip.

I tried the doorbell and knocked. I got no answer. I had a key which I used when she was out of the city, but the door was chained from the inside. I knew she must be in there. I called to her from the hallway entrance. Still no response. I tried to force the door open. The harder I tried, the tighter the chain became. I went down to my parked car and got out a part of the jack for changing a tire.

I pried the door open with the tire iron. As soon as I entered the apartment I walked toward her bedroom. I could see Dorothy's feet at the doorway of the bedroom. She was lying on the floor. I called softly, "Angel Face, Angel Face." I thought somehow she had fallen asleep on the floor.

She wore no clothes, but a blue scarf was wrapped about her head. She was cuddled with her face resting on her hands as if she was just sleeping.

Having reached her I called out and shook her shoulder to awaken her. She felt cold and it scared me. I looked at her again and softly said, "Angel Face," and reached for the phone and called her doctor. He said, "Call an ambulance right away. I'll be right there." I called the hospital where Dorothy and I were the evening before and they sent one. I covered Dorothy with a bath towel from the rack in the bathroom, then paced the floor continuously. I got a blanket from the hallway closet and covered her. The ambulance driver went from the bathroom to the phone. I asked him who he was calling. "The sheriff's office," he replied.

"How is she?" I asked. "Can't you do something for her?"

"She can't be helped by anyone," he replied. "She passed some time ago."

"Sheriff," he said, "we've got a cold one. Her name is Dorothy Dandridge." Her name was on an arm band put on in the hospital. "She's that colored singer, isn't she?"

Soon the police arrived with a representative from the coroner's office. Activity increased with each passing minute.

I remembered Dorothy told me that if anything ever happened, "I don't want anybody to look at me. I want to be cremated as soon as possible. I don't want any funeral. I want to give my eyes to the eye bank."

I made certain with a police sergeant's help that no press or others could see or photograph Dorothy. The detective and the coroner's office efficiently and politely did their work. I phoned Ruby Dandridge and I managed to get her to come to Dorothy's apartment with her dear friend, Dorothy Foster, without telling her that Dottie had passed. Ruby was in too much shock to make any funeral arrangements.

"Earl," she said, "you knew Dottie better than anyone, you know what she wants, you take care of everything."

I talked to Geri Branton, Dorothy's friend, and she called Angelus Mortuary. I later called Forest Lawn in Glendale, California, and arranged for meditation in the Little Chapel of the Flowers. Private cremation followed. I loved what Hilda Simms wrote for the Los Angeles Herald Examiner: "And when she had passed it was the ceasing of exquisite music.... Dorothy Dandridge has left us, but she walked in beauty ... regal as a queen."

I found out that she had been dead about two hours when I came into the house. She had bathed and applied powder and deodorant before dying. The question was, How had she died? Was it an accident? Was it natural death? Was it suicide?

Suicide usually requires there be a motive, and while she had many motives in the past, at this particular time of her life, in September of 1965, everything was going so well she had no motive. She had just recently said, "This is it. This time I'm going to make it bigger than ever."

She was to be paid $10,000 for her upcoming New York engagement and, in addition, $100,000 for the two Mexican pictures. Also I had an American western pending for her for which she was going to get an additional $50,000. Also she was writing her autobiography and the publisher, Bernard Geis, had given her a $10,000 advance.

One of Dorothy's last jobs was her first dramatic roles for the television show Blues For A Junkman, an episode for MGM-TV's "Cain's One Hundred" series which aired on NBC television. She played a glamorous night club singer struggling against odds to break the dope habit.

In Room 156 at the Hall of Justice there is a dossier of thirteen pages on Dorothy's death. It includes a Sheriff's report, the findings of the County Medical Examiner's toxicology lab and fingerprints. Dorothy was forty-two years old. It was the opinion of the Los Angeles County Coroner's office, determined immediately after her death, that Miss Dandridge had died of a rare embolism, blocking of the blood passages at the lungs and brain by tiny pieces of fat flaking from bone marrow in her fractured right foot.

The first coroner's report temporarily put an end to the widespread belief that she had taken her own life. The day after the coroner's verdict, final rites were held for her at Forest Lawn. Peter Lawford was at the funeral. He was the most prominent of the Hollywood people. Sidney Poitier phoned from Knabe, Utah. He wanted to be there but was unable to get to Los Angeles from his film location.

Soon after the funeral, Los Angeles County's chief medical examiner, Dr. Theodore Corphey, revealed that an exhaustive toxicological analysis by the Armed Forces Institute of Pathology had made another, new determination. The cause of Dorothy Dandridge's death was acute drug intoxication due to ingestion of Tofranil. That is the brand name of Imipramine Hydrochloride, a drug used to fight mental depression since it does not make people sleepy or forgetful as do some barbiturates. Imipramine Hydrochloride seemed to medical men an unlikely cause of accidental death.

Dr. Corphey had been vacationing in Hawaii at the time of Dorothy's death and the original cause report was issued by a subordinate. Due to the unusual finding, however, Dr. Corphey immediately decided the case needed further study and enlisted the aid of the more sophisticated laboratory techniques of the Armed Forces Institute of Pathology. Thus, the Tofranil discovery. The question of whether the death of Dorothy Dandridge was an accident or suicide was suddenly very much alive again, especially since the coroner's office admitted it had made no decision itself on the question.

As a result, a team of psychiatrists was assigned to explore Dorothy's past and thus perhaps provide an answer. It is what they call a psychological autopsy.

Of course, they came up with many disasters in her life, but that happens to many people in Hollywood. They weren't sure that would trigger a suicide. None of her close friends thought she committed suicide and I certainly don't.

I don't believe that Dorothy could have done that. Not when her career was booming. She was happy at the time.

Her good friend, attorney Leo Branton, said, "Dorothy had been on a downgrade. There were no pictures. Even her nightclub work had fallen off, but the last two months her career had taken a most dramatic turn. She had done phenomenally well wherever she appeared. She had signed new picture contracts. Her career had taken an upswing and so had her outlook on life."

Now the case is closed.

The Los Angeles County Health Department Certificate of Death states as follows: "Death was caused by acute intoxication. Ingestion of Tofranil.

Last occupation: Actress-singer.

Number of years in occupation: 39.

Age last birthday: 42 years.

Date of death: September 8, 1965."

On May 21, 1965, not long before she died, Dorothy handed me an envelope, which further added to the controversy over her death. On the envelope was written, "In case of my death—important." Inside the note read, "In case of my death—to whomever discovered it—don't remove anything I have on—scarf, gown or underwear. Cremate me right away. If I have anything, money, furniture, give it to my mother, Ruby

Dandridge. She will know what to do. Dorothy
Dandridge."

Many people, at first, interpreted this as a suicide
note, not unnaturally, because of the wording. It was
only after I was able to prove that Dorothy had given
me the note months before her death that it was offi-
cially discounted.

Was it a premonition of death? I don't think so.
Dorothy always had a morbid fascination with death
and thought of what might happen after her own passing.

The note was finally interpreted as merely instructions for her burial and the disposition of her posses-
sions.

But Dorothy Dandridge died too young. She was
on the way up again. I believe that she would not only
have regained the heights but would have risen even
higher. It was not to be.

One writer expressed best what everyone felt who
knew Dorothy: "If you've never been in love, she
makes you want to be; and if you're already in love, she
makes you want to stay that way."

Introducing
**Dorothy Dandridge
The Film With Halle Berry**

Introducing
Dorothy Dandridge
The Film

Essay by Marianne Ruuth

Photographs in the section by
Sidney Baldwin

It happened one night in Cleveland. A strikingly beautiful, bright, sensitive nineteen-year-old girl came upon the film *Carmen Jones* with Dorothy Dandridge, Harry Belafonte and Pearl Bailey on television. She sat up straight as she watched a full-bodied performance by a truly exciting actress. Who is—or was—Dorothy Dandridge?! And how come I don't know about her? she asked herself. I know of Marilyn Monroe, Grace Kelly, Ava Gardner...but not Dorothy Dandridge! Why?! How is this possible?

Not yet knowing her own future as an actress but disheartened at not having been aware of this remarkable woman and her contributions, she began reading all she could about Dorothy, growing more and more amazed, both by what she learned and by the fact that there was so little information about her, even in Cleveland. After all, Dorothy Dandridge was from Cleveland, born on November 9, 1922. She went on to experience tremendous success nationally and internationally, against all odds, and yet somehow became the invisible woman in film history. Harry Belafonte once called her "the right person in the right place at the wrong time..."

Before long, Halle Berry from Cleveland did indeed become an actress in her own right and thereby part of the legacy of Dorothy Dandridge.

Fast forward to the late 1980s. Halle Berry was still relatively unknown when Vincent Cirrincione recognized a huge and unique talent and became her manager.

Echoing the sentiments of Dorothy Dandridge, Halle Berry would talk to him about the difficulties of being a black actress, the limitations, the constant struggle. As her career flourished and she reached a point where she had more clout in the business, they agreed she had to create her own opportunities. "Find a project you really want to do," said he at one time.

Her face brightened, and she revealed that what she wanted to do more than almost anything was to bring the life of Dorothy Dandridge to the screen.

Vince remembered back to his own childhood. Even as a boy of ten, he had been aware of Dorothy Dandridge and felt the thrill of her beauty and personality. And so a seven-year quest was initiated, one that would take all the energy and passion he and his young client could muster. With never flagging intensity, Cirrincione believed the Dandridge story with Halle Berry was something people needed to see. "For a lot of reasons," he says. "Not only did Dandridge have to fight against racism, she had to fight against her own demons."

While making other films, Halle Berry kept her dream alive. Relentless and unstoppable, she never considered giving it up—because paying homage to Dorothy Dandridge and recognizing her significance was something she knew she had to do.

The Dandridge spirit must have been in the air because suddenly several talented actresses announced their wish to play the actress/singer/dancer who has been called the Jackie Robinson of the film industry, as she with talent, determination and ladylike dignity broke several more or less visible barriers. Existing books about her were optioned, plans were made, and the media played guessing games as to who would be the first to realize the Dorothean dream.

Now we know the answer—Halle Berry!

However, it didn't happen in the blink of an eye. First there was the matter of options. The book she and Vince wanted was this very one, written by Earl Mills, Dandridge's manager who loved her with all his heart almost from the day he met her in 1951.

Vince made the first of many calls to Earl Mills who was now living in Palm Springs and learned that Mills' book had been optioned by a well-known singer/actress. Vince kept checking, maintaining a relationship with Mills, and eventually the option ran out, although now someone else wanted it so Holloway House publisher Bentley Morriss along with Earl Mills had to be pursued and convinced that the Vince/Halle team was perfect. Another executive producer, Josh Mauer, had by this time been brought in to join Vince and Halle, and the work began in earnest.

An extensive pitching round to the movie studios brought a chorus of negative responses. "A bio pic of a black actress in the 1950's?! Not interested," said they.

So the trio went to HBO, the cable company that loves films and dares to go where others fear, including having no hesitation about African American-themed projects. Of course, first the powers-that-be there also had to be educated about Dorothy Dandridge and then convinced that everything would be of the highest quality, beginning with the script, the director, and not the least the star. The development period stretched over a couple of years.

In retrospect it seems clear and absolutely logical that the final ingredients in this venture would add up to success but in the early stages there were many ques-

Halle Berry as Dorothy Dandridge, the club singer.

tions, long discussions, numerous meetings and end-less matters to work out and agree upon. As Vince puts an old show business truth: "Success has many fathers; failure has none."

WORDS BECOMING PICTURES...

A young writer, Shonda Rhimes, although still in her twenties, was more knowledgeable than most about Dorothy Dandridge even before this project.

"But then my parents are academicians and to them she is part of history. I actually wrote a paper on her in college," says she, acknowledging that it is far from an easy task to put a tumultuous life into two movie hours. She differentiates between the movie and the story of Dorothy's life in bookform: "Making a movie is like taking a snapshot. You get an image of someone but you don't know everything. The beauty of a book is that it tells you other things, things a movie cannot. It's like reading someone's letter as opposed to looking at the pictures they sent along with it."

Shonda went to Palm Springs and spent several days with Earl Mills, finding him "wonderful and inter-esting. It was sadly fascinating, too... because it's as if time stopped for him when Dorothy died. Emotions would cross his face as if it all happened yesterday. To me that's absolute love," says she.

The director, Martha Coolidge, was carefully picked after lengthy considerations (male or female? white or black?), the choice based on her past films, especially her exquisite work in the motion picture *Rambling Rose*. She found Earl Mills' book lending itself exceptionally well to the making of a movie. "Lots of details and although what he says is colored by his emotions, you can hear that she told him these stories, you can hear her voice. I liked that."

She adds that the relationship between Earl Mills

and Dorothy "is a basis for our entire movie which is about Dorothy's endless and futile search for love. Toward the end she might have realized that there was one man who loved her, meaning Earl—even though she could never be in love with him."

Coolidge's personal memory of Dorothy Dandridge stems from seeing her singing on the Ed Sullivan Show, a program her family used to watch. Even as a child she was touched by the persona, sensuality and complexity of Dorothy—and today she feels this movie is important.

"Certainly and without question because she was black and because of all the breakthroughs she made but I also think it's one of the most interesting stories I've ever encountered of beautiful women victimized by our industry. So in addition to being extremely socially significant, on a psychological level I feel her story is certainly as interesting as the stories of Judy Garland or Marilyn Monroe with an added exploitation factor because she was black. As a woman, she has a great deal to tell us about the masochistic streak women have when facing limits in a business where historically women have been terribly limited. Those limits are worse when you are a black woman. The story illustrates how we as women have a tendency to turn on ourselves rather than strike out."

Did anything surprise her as she delved into the story?

"Yes. I was extremely surprised to find out that Dorothy's mother was a lesbian. I don't think many people know that. Her mother actually dumped her father for a woman—and told Dorothy that her father left her. It was the basic lie in the family with the father depicted as no good when in fact he was very stable and middle-class, owned a good business and always wanted his daughters. Generally, the story is more contemporary than I thought before entering into it.

"I was also shocked at the things I learned about

The Dandridge Sisters as played in the film by

Sharon Brown, Halle Berry and CyndaWilliams.

discrimination in the 40s and 50s. Even more shocking is the fact that some of this hasn't changed."

The film provides no lengthy forays into Dorothy Dandridge's childhood as it starts basically when she is eighteen and ends when she died at age forty-two.

Martha Coolidge discusses the special challenges involved in making a film about someone's life. To avoid piling one event on the other, making it episodic or too much like a documentary, she came up with idea of a *frame*.

"One long phone call! I kept in mind that it's about a search for love and identity and that, later in life, Dorothy became an insomniac who could stay up all night, calling friends. Essentially the movie is Dorothy talking on the phone to her best friend, Geri Branton, trying to make sense out of her life and her pursuit of love and coming to grips with the accomplishments in her career. Being able to jump around in her life as we bring to life the memories that relate to her phone conversation made the story cohesive."

THE PLAYERS...

Both Shonda Rhimes and Martha Coolidge have many adjective-laden comments when speaking of Halle Berry, both as an actress with strong creative powers of transformation and as a human being.

"Kind and generous and spirited," says Shonda with emphasis. "A rare phenomenon in this business because she is very beautiful, very talented and obviously famous, yet she is uninterested in her image and all the crap that goes along with it. She is interested in being a person, and I really like that. And I have never seen anybody work harder."

There are two basic kinds of actors—those who strive always to serve the story and those who let the story serve them and their talent.

Halle Berry, who stars as Dorothy Dandridge,
and Martha Coolidge, the director of the film.

"With Halle, it's about the work," says Shonda. "Forgive me if I sound self-centered but she struck me as having a writer's spirit. Writers spend their time living the lives of their characters. I lived within and with Dorothy, thought about her, dreamt about her, at times felt haunted by her—and so did Halle who managed to embody Dorothy wonderfully. There were many amazing moments. Once while recreating a *Carmen Jones* scene and finishing touches were done to Halle's makeup, she was standing there, backlit, silhouetted, and suddenly looking so much like Dorothy that it was eerie."

Martha Coolidge and Halle Berry did not know each other before this film, and Martha laughs when remembering their first encounter at a production meeting. "She was very feisty," says she who exhibits a great deal of the same quality herself. "I took to her right away. She's a strong woman, and I like that."

Her first impression was strengthened as the work went on. "Halle is dedicated, a total professional, extremely talented and with incredible depth. She lived up to enormous challenges every minute of every day, as she made Dorothy her own. She was exceptional to work with—she is one of the finest people I know in this business. She has standards, her feet are firmly planted on the ground and she treats people well."

She also reveals that excerpts from Dorothy Dandridge films shown are actual re-creations with Halle and the other actors. No clips were used at all.

Halle Berry is one of the executive producers on the show, and in her case it was certainly no vanity position. "We tried to avoid relying on her during the shooting," says Martha Coolidge, "because she had to be immersed in her role but this is an ambitious movie and there were some tough choices to make during actual production. When those had to be made, Halle was right there. She fought hard for what was right and really helped helm some of the truly hard deci-

Loretta Devine as Mother Ruby Dandridge.

sions that had to be made."

What was it really like to get under the skin of the complicated Dorothy Dandridge?

"The biggest revelation was how much we are alike," says Halle Berry. "It was almost frightening. Many of her issues felt familiar to me, being issues I have been dealing with in my own life. I didn't realize until I played her how much of a masochist she was— and how sad. She had so much, being beautiful and talented and glamorous, but she always had a sadness about her. And a sort of unfulfilled feeling... It fascinated me that somebody could have so much and yet never feel really happy. It became almost therapy as it made me realize that this cannot happen to me, that her story can never be my story. It reminded me that happiness is found in the small things in life. It's about people, about family and about loving yourself. She made me take a look at all that for myself."

She says the town of Hollywood, meaning the entertainment industry, has not really changed that much.

"They didn't know what to do with her and they don't know what to do with me. It's frustrating and brings about a profound kind of pain that's hard to explain. Most don't realize it or don't believe it to be true. They don't realize what it's like to be a black actress. Even to make this story was hard. With all your love and all your passion, you have to work enormously hard and create your own opportunities that challenge and inspire you."

She also learned something else that will impact her future. "I discovered that I want to go on producing and not always be the dancing bear!"

"While in actual production, I had to split my time between being actress and producer but before and after the shoot, I was wearing my producer's hat. Before we filmed I involved myself in the script, in hiring Martha and so on... and then during post-produc-

Halle Berry as Dorothy Dandridge and Brent Spiner as Earl Mills.

tion I participated in the discussions and decisions about music, editing, marketing, the poster... HBO has been great, allowing me to act seriously as producer, valuing my opinions and listening to my creative input. I wanted so much to make this the best project possible, knowing it would be scrutinized, especially in view of several other wonderful women wanting to play Dorothy. Since I am the first out of the gate, I wanted it to be really special."

Her only problem might be to find something worthwhile to do after this (not unlike Dorothy Dandridge's problem after *Carmen Jones* and her Academy Award nomination).

"My dream came true and I got to play a full, rich character that allowed me to explore all my assets as an actress. So what can compare with this? How often do you get to use every part of your instrument, emotionally and physically?"

She emphasizes that there is also humor in the movie as it is more a celebration of Dorothy's life than a tragic story.

"That was my vision always. One possible criticism could be that someone might feel she dies too quickly—but we wanted the movie to show how she lived, not just how she died. The death comes because that's history. She is found dead, naked on the bathroom floor, just like it happened but we don't focus on that. The film is about her life and her legacy and the contributions she made. Even after we show her death, the movie still ends with her dancing and singing. That's the last image you see of her and that's really how I want people to remember her."

Halle Berry spoke to as many people as she could about Dorothy and says that the greatest insights were given to her by Sidney Poitier (he and Dorothy did *Porgy and Bess* together) and by Dorothy's closest friend, Geri Branton (who personified what a true friend is—never judging, always there).

"Both said the same thing, and that made me confident that I had to find a way to bring it to the screen. They said that Dorothy had a real vulnerability about her that was there every minute of every day, in every way, in everything she did. She was somehow on the verge of tears, of breaking down, of being emotional—something vulnerable was always happening inside her. I kept that in the back of my mind always, and Geri told me, 'If you can do that, then you'll capture the essence of who Dorothy was.'"

Many others remember most clearly how dazzled they were by Dorothy. Halle spoke with Diahann Carroll "but she was so young and was just mesmerized by Dorothy's beauty, her vitality and talent—she just aspired to be like her."

Another thing that Halle had to keep in mind as an underlying key to character was Dorothy's everpresent sense of guilt. "It was a burden she carried her whole life, the guilt about her severely retarded daughter Harolyn, called Lynn. Did she in some way cause the little one's brain damage? Was she not a good enough mother, having to leave her in order to work?"

Before the filming, Halle tried to find Lynn. "The state institution she was in burned down several years ago and nobody knows where Lynn went afterwards. So she is lost right now, if she is even still living. We weren't able to find out."

It was painful for Halle to recreate the racism of the time and what black artists went through. "They could perform in a club but they couldn't use the bathroom, they couldn't eat in the restaurant. They could perform but they couldn't talk to the patrons. And there was that time when Dorothy is in Las Vegas and the hotel manager tells her that she can't swim in the pool and if she does, the pool has to be drained. She actually sticks her foot in the pool, and the next evening she sees that the pool has been drained..."

Halle Berry dancing with Klaus Maria Brandauer.

Brandauer plays Otto Preminger in the film.

LOOKING FOR THE RIGHT MAN...

Speaking of the men in Dorothy's life outside of the ever-present Earl Mills, Halle says they focused on the three they felt impacted her life most: The dancer Harold Nicholas, her first husband who wasn't really ready for marriage, the director Otto Preminger, and the manipulative Jack Dennison, an unfortunate choice of husband.

"Otto Preminger is at the core of what the movie is about—the success of *Carmen Jones*, her Oscar nomination, the powerful Otto being her lover. I think it represented the high, the pivotal point of her life and then, quickly, it all turned and became her downfall. Otto left her. She was nominated but didn't win and afterwards had a hard time getting work."

In the film, dynamic director Otto Preminger is played by Austrian Klaus Maria Brandauer, an acclaimed stage actor throughout the German-speaking world. With *Mephisto* in 1981, he became internationally known. He was then nominated for an Academy Award as best supporting actor for his performance in the Meryl Streep/Robert Redford starrer *Out of Africa* in 1985 and made an impressive debut as film director in 1990 (with *Seven Minutes*). Brandauer might be one of the utterly few actors who could capture the essence of Otto Preminger.

"He has that bigger-than-life aura that I've been told Otto Preminger had. He sort of fills up the whole room," says Halle.

Otto Preminger was eighteen years Dorothy's senior. Although he was Jewish, he started out playing Nazis in Hollywood. The movie *Laura* (1944) put him on the map as a director and earned him his first Academy Award nomination. His film *The Moon Is Blue* in 1953 unleashed a storm of controversy (imagine, they used words such as "pregnant" and "virgin" in it!), and he entered into the world of drug addicts (another taboo subject) with *The Man With the Golden Arm*. *Carmen Jones* was of course a big hit—while *Porgy and Bess* did less well for him, although Dorothy won praise for what she brought to the role of Bess.

On movie sets, Preminger was known as Otto the Terrible because of his temper and his frequently cruel methods to get certain performances out of his actors.

Undeniably, he was courageous in his work, daring to go where nobody else had gone, taking risks, offering jobs to black-listed talents and so on. In his private life, he might have been less willing to take some risks—such as marrying a black woman...

It was actually quite a coup to get Brandauer for this role. It was Martha Coolidge's first casting decision, and she wrote him a personal letter, sending him extensive material on herself, Halle Berry and Otto Preminger. The actor expressed interest but there were severe complications because he was shooting a movie about Rembrandt simultaneously.

"A difficult deal was made where finally he could give us twelve, thirteen days including travel. We had seventeen days of shooting scheduled for him but I condensed everything because I felt he was worth it and everybody agreed," says Coolidge. "With a limited number of days and no leeway anywhere, if anybody had taken ill, we would have been in big trouble. But Klaus came in, was fantastic in the movie, fantastic to work with, and everybody loved him."

The fact that Brandauer was to play Preminger was a big drawing card for the actor who plays Earl Mills, Brent Spiner. Some might know him mainly as Data in the *Star Trek* series and movies but, to quote Martha Coolidge, Spiner is "a very gifted actor whom I wanted from the very beginning; he is kind of a best-kept secret, not known to many in an obvious way because he disappears into his parts. You know him as Data or the crazy scientist in *Independence Day* or the doctor in

Left to right: Obba Babatunde as Harold Nicholas,
Dorothy Dandridge's first husband, Halle Berry

Darrian C. Ford as Fayard Nicholas and
Tamara Taylor as his wife Geri Nicholas-Branton.

Phenomenon—and he was my bad guy in *Out to Sea*. He has done musicals on Broadway and a lot more. A wonderful contributor to the film, an actor with excellent taste, and he and Halle worked long and hard on their relationship which is not one of passion but of subtle caring on his part. She appreciates him and yet doesn't appreciate him. But truly he loves her totally. He wanted to marry her. She was his life."

Having always been a film buff, Brent Spiner knew quite a bit about Dorothy Dandridge. "I remember when she died although I was a kid at the time. The papers said it was because she had hurt her toe, and that really scared me."

He gives his view of Earl Mills. "Basically a guy who is desperately in love, almost from the moment he meets her. In the first couple of scenes, he seems to be in control. He is an agent, he's a manager, he's a businessman, pretty sure of himself, doing pretty well. I think he feels good about himself. Then he meets her and relinquishes control almost immediately. He will do anything for her, whatever she wants. Little by little, he gives it all up for her, basically losing himself, becoming someone who serves someone else."

It might sound as a reversal of traditional male/female roles. How does an actor approach such a character?

Brent Spiner, who has a philosophical bent, says that if he tries to find a theme in his work "and it's really stretching to find a commonality in my work because I try to do something different every time out, but the most common thread is that I tend to play men who want to be something they are not. Earl wants to be the center of her life, and he simply is not. She doesn't see it. She doesn't really, really see him. And when she possibly begins to see him more clearly toward the end, realizing the difference between the destructive men in her life and this man who doesn't want to destroy her but only to save her... then she dies."

He learned more from watching Earl Mills than from actually talking to him. "He's an old man now but still dressed to the nines and making a wonderful presentation. That's how it was in the 1950s, it was about image... presentation..."

During the filming Earl Mills brought about thirteen big boxes of mementos from his life with Dorothy. Every scrap of paper, everything she wrote, every telegram, every letter, every photo, several dresses and outfits, even pill bottles with her name on them.

"It was 45 years ago but he still has everything," comments Spiner who actually acquired a photocopy of the contract between Earl and Dorothy. "He brought all this with him from Palm Springs, and we asked if we could keep some of it to look through and then deliver back to him the next day. No, he refused to leave it. So HBO put him up in a hotel in town so he was near the stuff at all times."

Brent Spiner is delighted to speak about Halle whom he calls "absolutely brilliant in this movie. I think she achieves everything she was going for. A real triumph for her. She is spectacular. She has the gamut to play, every possible performance thing you can do. She goes emotionally and physically from A to Z. She acts, she sings, she dances—she even learned to tap in no time and, believe me, tap is not easy. She does everything a human being can possibly do and she does it exceedingly well. She has been terrific in everything she has done before but this goes way, way beyond... She didn't hold back in any sense, and it paid off."

He did see a lot of Dorothy in Halle.

"She has experienced many of the same things. Also the fact that she is incredibly beautiful. Whichever angle you look at Dorothy, she is beautiful. Same with Halle. Working with Halle right now is like working with Elizabeth Taylor when she was that age. You look at the monitor and realize that the camera can search all day and is never going to find a bad angle on that face.

Earl Mills, Dorothy Dandridge's long-time manager and the author of the book

with Halle Berry and Producer Vincent Cirrincione

Add to that Halle's remarkable insight and intuition, qualities I believe she shares with Dorothy..."

Being a great admirer of Klaus Maria Brandauer's work, Spiner was thrilled being given the chance of working with the man he calls "one of the great actors of the world, the Marlon Brando of Europe, actually." Aware of Brandauer having a certain reputation of being difficult (a label sometimes stuck on those who desire perfection), he is happy to report that the actor turned out to be "generous, charming, personable, cooperative and wonderfully easy to work with."

Of course, in the film, Otto is the one who usurps Earl whom he saw as ineffectual and not useful at all.

"Earl was Dorothy's support system, and Otto took that away from him," notes Spiner.

He goes on to say that the entire cast was exceptional.

"Everybody approached the work with passion, everybody felt the importance of the film. I think, as important as it is to remember Dorothy and what her experience was like, it is equally important to take a look at it through the glasses of today and ask: Is it really that different? It is different, yes, but is it *that* different? Because I think our evolution is only superficial. We are involved in finding all kinds of creature comforts and making our lives more fun but deep, deep down, I'm not sure we have grown much at all. When I look at this film and at Dorothy's experience, I guarantee you there are a lot of female black entertainers who have just as difficult a time today, who go through the same agonies and horrible humiliations that Dorothy did. This film reminds us that this was happening forty years ago and still is."

For the role of Dorothy Dandridge's first husband, Harold Nicholas, half of the dancing Nicholas Brothers, was chosen one of the truly exciting actors on stage and screen, Obba Babatunde, a Tony award nominee (for the original *Dreamgirls* production).

"He was so much fun, so spirited, such a showman. He really brought Harold to life," says Shonda Rhimes.

The older Nicholas brother, Fayard (Darrian C. Ford in the film), is still alive and came on the set, checking out the dance numbers, and when he pronounced them good, Halle Berry knew they were.

There were high marks from all involved for everyone in the cast.

About Cynda Williams who is portraying Dorothy's sister Vivian, Brent Spiner notes: "Cynda was great. There was a scene in a club where she flips out completely and lets Dorothy have it. An amazing sequence."

Loretta Devine plays Dorothy's mother, Ruby, who created a career of her own in Hollywood as a movie and radio comedienne while D.B. Sweeney fills the role as Dorothy's last husband, Jack Dennison. LaTanya Richardson is seen as Aunt Neva, the woman who replaced Ruby's husband and became the girls' strict mentor/guardian, and Sharon Brown appears as the young Etta Jones, whom Ruby had added to form the singing trio, The Dandridge Sisters, in the early 1930s.

Halle Berry spent a lot of time talking to Geri Branton, once Dorothy's sister-in-law and then forever her closest friend. (In the film, Geri Nicholas-Branton is played by Tamara Taylor.)

"Getting the woman's point of view gave me a different perspective. For instance, while the men who are still alive do not feel that Dorothy committed suicide, Geri believes she did. I asked and she said, 'Most definitely. Dotty could never have been an older woman. I couldn't see her getting around in a walker like I do.' Which is why we have a line in the movie where Dorothy says, 'I'm not going to get old. I'm going to stay young and beautiful to the day I die.'"

TO YOU FROM HALLE BERRY AND COMPANY...
AND FROM EARL MILLS, THE MAN WHO LOVED
DOROTHY DANDRIDGE UNCONDITIONALLY...

Halle Berry feels strongly that this is a human
story, sometimes sad but also inspiring.
"If you're black, there's a lot to identify with—
from pain to pride. But even if you are not black and
can't relate personally to the black issues, there is the
woman issue. And if you're not a woman, there is the
human issue, there are those men, those relationships.
I feel anyone can identify with the story. It has something to give everyone... and that's what we wanted!"

So step into a magnetic field of energy, powered by
love. A man's love without limits, a woman searching
for love, artists expressing their love through communication and creation as they tell this particular story—
and may it create a spark in you to live and to love,
with curiosity and enthusiasm...

HBO Pictures presents
An Esparza/Katz Production
in association with Berry/Cirrincione

A Martha Coolidge Film

Halle Berry

INTRODUCING
DOROTHY DANDRIDGE

Brent Spiner, Obba Babatunde, Loretta Devine,
Cynda Williams, LaTanya Richardson, Tamara
Taylor, Alexis Carrington
and
Klaus Maria Brandauer as Otto Preminger

Music by Elmer Bernstein
Music Supervisor Robin Urdang
Editor Alan Heim, A.C.E.
Production Designer James Spencer
Director of Photography Robert Greenberg, A.S.C.
Produced by Larry Y. Albucher
Executive Producers Robert Katz, Moctesuma
Esparza, Joshua D. Maurer
Vincent Cirrincione and Halle Berry
Screenplay by Shonda Rhimes and Scott Abbott
Based on the book "Dorothy Dandridge"
by Earl Mills
Directed by Martha Coolidge

Soundtrack available on RCA Victor Records

INDEX

*Earl Mills was Dorothy
Dandridge's manager and
friend during her successful
professional life.
He celebrated victories with
her and suffered with her
when times were tough.
Their relationship often
bordered on the romantic.
Earl wrote this biography
as a labor of love. The love
shines through.*